# MORE THAN A
# CONVENIENT
# MARRIAGE?

# MORE THAN A CONVENIENT MARRIAGE?

BY

DANI COLLINS

MILLS
BOON®

First published in Great Britain 2013
by Mills & Boon, an imprint of Harlequin (UK) Limited,
Large Print edition 2014
Eton House, 18-24 Paradise Road,
Richmond, Surrey, TW9 1SR

© 2013 Dani Collins

ISBN: 978 0 263 24043 6

Printed and bound in Great Britain
by CPI Antony Rowe, Chippenham, Wiltshire

For my sisters,
'cause they live far away and I miss 'em.

# CHAPTER ONE

GIDEON VOZARAS USED all his discipline to keep his foot light on the accelerator as he followed the rented car, forcing himself to maintain an unhurried pace along the narrow island road while he gripped the wheel in white-knuckled fists. When the other car parked outside the palatial gate of an estate, he pulled his own rental onto the shoulder a discreet distance back then stayed in his vehicle to see if the other driver noticed. As he cut the engine, the AC stopped. Heat enveloped him.

*Welcome to hell.*

He hated Greece at the best of times and today was predicted to be one of the hottest on record. The air shimmered under the relentless sun and it wasn't even ten o'clock yet. But the weather was barely worth noticing.

The gates of the estate were open. The other car could have driven straight through and up to the house, but stayed parked outside. He watched the female driver emerge and take a moment to consider the unguarded entrance. Her shoulders gave a lift and drop as though she screwed up her courage before she took action and walked in.

As she disappeared between imposing brick posts, Gideon left his own car and followed at a measured pace, gut knotting with every step. Outrage stung his veins.

He wanted to believe that wasn't his wife, but there was no mistaking Adara Vozaras. Not for him. Maybe her tourist clothes of flip-flops, jeans chopped above the knees, a sleeveless top and a pair of pigtails didn't fit her usual professional élan, but he knew that backside. The tug it caused in his blood was indisputable. No other woman made an immediate sexual fire crackle awake in him like this. His relentless hunger for Adara had always been his cross to bear and today it was particularly unwelcome.

*Spending the week with her mother.* This ain't Chatham, sweetheart.

He paused as he came alongside her car, glancing inside to see a map of the island on the passenger seat. A logo in its corner matched the hotel he'd been told she was booked into. And now she was advising her lover where to meet her? Walking bold as you please up his million-dollar driveway to his billion-dollar house? The only clue to the estate's ownership, the shields welded to the gate, were turned back against the brick wall that fenced the estate from the road.

Gideon's entire body twitched with an urge to slip his reins of control. He was not a poor man. He'd got past envying other men their wealth once he'd acquired a certain level of his own. Nevertheless, a niggle of his dock-rat inferiority complex wormed to life as he took in what he could see of the shoreline property that rolled into a vineyard and orange grove. The towering stone house, three stories with turrets on each corner, belonged on an English estate, not a Greek island. It was twenty bedrooms minimum. If this was the owner's weekend retreat, he was an obscenely rich man.

Not that Adara needed a rich man. She had grown up wanting for nothing. She had a fortune in her own right plus half of Gideon's, so what was the attraction here?

*Sex.*

The insidious whisper formed a knot of betrayal behind his breastbone. Was this why she hadn't shared that stacked body of hers with him for weeks? His hands curled into fists as he tried to swallow back his gall.

Dreading what he might see as he looked to the front door, he shifted for a full view. Adara had paused halfway to the house to speak with a gardener. A truck overflowing with landscaping tools was parked midway up the driveway and workers were crawling like bees over the blooming gardens.

The sun seared the back of Gideon's neck, strong enough to burn through his shirt to his shoulders, making sweat pool between his shoulder blades and trickle annoyingly down his spine.

They had arrived early this morning, Adara off the ferry, Gideon following in a powerboat he was "test-piloting." She'd been driving a car she'd rented in Athens. His rental had been negotiated at the marina, but the island was small. It hadn't surprised him when she'd driven right past the nose of his car as he had turned onto the main road.

No, the surprise had been the call thirty-six hours previously when their travel agent had dialed his mobile by mistake. Ever the survivor,

Gideon had thought quickly. He'd mentioned that he'd like to surprise his wife by joining her and within seconds, Gideon had had all the details of Adara's clandestine trip.

Well, not all. He didn't know whom she was here to see or how she'd met her mystery man. *Why was she doing this when he gave her everything she asked for?*

He watched Adara's slender neck bow in disappointment. Ha. The bastard wasn't home. Grimly satisfied, Gideon folded his arms and waited for his wife.

Adara averted her gaze from the end of the driveway where the sun was glancing off her rented car and piercing straight into her eyes.

The grounds of this estate were an infinitely more beautiful place to look anyway. Groomed lawn gently rolled into vineyards, and a white sand beach gleamed below. The dew was off the grass, the air moving hotly up from the water with a tang of salt on it. Everything was brilliant and elevating.

Perhaps that was just her frame of mind, but it was a refreshing change from depression and anxiety and rejection. She paused to savor the first optimistic moment she'd had in weeks. Looking out on the horizon where Mediterranean blue met cloudless sky, she sighed in contentment. She hadn't felt so relaxed since… Since ever. Early childhood maybe. Very early childhood.

And it wouldn't last. A sick ache opened in her belly as she remembered Gideon. And his PA.

Not yet, she reminded herself. This week was hers. She was stealing it for herself and her brother. If he returned. The gardener had said a few days, but Adara's research had put Nico on this island all week, so he obviously changed his schedule rapidly. Hopefully he'd return as suddenly as he'd left.

*Just call him,* she cajoled herself, but after this many years she wasn't sure he'd know who she was or want to hear from her. He'd never picked up the telephone himself. If he refused to speak to her, well, a throb of hurt pulsed in her throat as she contemplated that. She swallowed it back. She just wanted to see him, look into his eyes and learn why he'd never come home or spoken to her or her younger brothers again.

Another cleansing breath, but this one a little more troubled as she turned toward her car again.

She was crestfallen Nico wasn't here, not that she'd meant to come like this to his house, first thing on arrival, but her room at the hotel hadn't been ready. On impulse she'd decided to at least find the estate, and then the gates had been open and she'd been drawn in. Now she had to wait—

"Lover boy not home?"

The familiar male voice stopped her heart and jerked her gaze up from the chevron pattern in the cobblestones to the magnificence that was her husband. Swift, fierce attraction sliced through her, sharp and disarming as always.

Not a day passed that she didn't wonder how she'd landed such a smoking-hot man. He was shamelessly handsome, his features even and just hard enough to be undeniably masculine. He rarely smiled, but he didn't have to charm when his sophistication and intelligence commanded such respect. The sheer physical presence of him quieted a room. She always thought of him as a purebred stallion, outwardly still and disciplined, but with an invisible energy and power that warned he could explode any second.

*Don't overlook resourceful,* she thought acridly. How else had he turned up half a world from where she'd thought he would be, when she'd taken pains to keep her whereabouts strictly confidential?

Fortunately, Adara had a lot of experience hiding visceral reactions like instant animal attraction and guilty alarm. She kept her sunglasses on and willed her pulse to slow, keeping her limbs loose and her body language unreadable.

"What are you doing here?" she asked with a composed lift of her chin. "Lexi said you would be in Chile." Lexi's tone still grated, so proprietary over Gideon's schedule, so pitying as she had looked upon the ignorant wife who not only failed as a woman biologically, but no longer interested her husband sexually. Adara had wanted to erase the woman's superior smile with a swipe of her manicured nails.

"Let's turn that question around, shall we?" Gideon strolled with deadly negligence around the front of her car.

Adara had never been afraid of him, not physically, not the way she had been of her father, but somewhere along the line Gideon had developed the power to hurt her with a look or a word, without even trying, and that scared her. She steeled herself against him, but her nerves fried with the urge to flee.

She made herself stand her ground and find the reliable armor of civility she'd grown as self-defense long ago. It had always served her well in her dealings with this man, even allowing her to engage with him intimately without losing herself. Still, she wanted higher, thicker invisible walls. Her reasons for coming to Greece were too private to share, carrying as they did such a heavy risk of rejection. That's why she hadn't told him or anyone else where she was going. Having him turn up like this put her on edge, internally windmilling her arms as she tried to hang on to unaffected nonchalance.

"I'm here on personal business," she said in a dismissive tone that didn't invite discussion.

He, in turn, should have given her his polite nod of acknowledgment that always drove home how supremely indifferent he was to what happened in her world. It might hurt a little, but far better to have her trials and triumphs disregarded than dissected and diminished.

While she, as was her habit, wouldn't bother repeating a question he had ignored, even though she really did want to know how and why he'd followed her.

No use changing tactics now, she thought. With a little adherence to form they could end this relationship as dispassionately as they'd started it.

That gave her quite a pang and oddly, even though his body language was as neutral as always, and his expression remained impassive as he squinted against the brightness of the day, she again had the sense of that coiled force drawing more tightly inside him. When he spoke, his words were even, yet she sensed an underlying ferocity.

"I can see how personal it is. Who is he?"

Her heart gave a kick. Gideon rarely got angry and even more rarely showed it. He certainly never directed dark energy at her, but his accusation made her unaccountably defensive.

She told herself not to let his jab pierce her shell, but his charge was a shock and she couldn't believe his gall. The man was banging his secretary in the most clichéd of affairs, yet he had the nerve to dog her all the way to Greece to accuse *her* of cheating?

Fortunately, she knew from experience you didn't provoke a man in a temper. Hiding her indignation behind cool disdain, she calmly corrected his assumption. "*He* has a wife and new baby—"

Gideon's drawled sarcasm cut her off. "Cheating on one spouse wasn't enough, you have to go for two and ruin the life of a child into the mix?"

*Since when do you care about children?*

She bit back the question, but a fierce burn flared behind her eyes, completely unwanted right now when she needed to keep her head. The back of her throat stung, making her voice thick. She hoped he'd put it down to ire, not heartbreak.

"As I said, Lexi assured me you had appointments in Chile. '*We* will be flying into Valparaiso,' she told me. '*We* will be staying in the family suite at the Makricosta Grand.'" Adara impassively pronounced what Lexi hadn't said, but what had been in the woman's eyes and supercilious smile. "'*We* will be wrecking your bed and calling your staff for breakfast in the morning.' Who is cheating on whom?"

She was proud of her aloof delivery, but her underlying resentment was still more emotion than she'd ever dared reveal around him. She couldn't help it. His adultery was a blow she hadn't seen coming and she was always on guard for unearned strikes. Always. Somehow she'd convinced herself she could trust him and if she was angry with anyone, it was with herself for being so blindly oblivious. She was so furious she was having a hard time hiding that she was trembling, but she ground her teeth and willed her muscles to let go of the tension and her blood to stop boiling.

He didn't react. If she fought a daily battle to keep her emotions in reserve, his inner thoughts and feelings were downright nonexistent. His voice was crisp and glacial when he said, "Lexi did not say that because it's not true. And why would you care if she did? *We* aren't wrecking any beds, are we?"

*Ask me why,* she wanted to charge, but the words and the reason stayed bottled so deep and hard inside her she couldn't speak.

Grief threatened to overtake her then. Hopelessness crept in and defeat struck like a gong. It sent an arctic chill into her, blessed ice that let her freeze out the pain and ignore the humiliation. She wanted it all to go away.

"I want a divorce," she stated, heart throbbing in her throat.

For a second, the world stood still. She wasn't sure if she'd actually said it aloud and he didn't move, as though he either hadn't heard, or couldn't comprehend.

Then he drew in a long, sharp inhale. His shoulders pulled back and he stood taller.

Oh, God. Everything in her screamed, *Retreat.* She ducked her head and circled him, aiming for her car door.

He put out a hand and her blood gave a betraying leap. She quickly tamped down the hunger and yearning, embracing hatred instead.

"Don't think for a minute I'll let you touch me," she warned in a voice that grated.

"Right. Touching is off limits. I keep forgetting."

A stab of compunction, of incredible sadness and longing to be understood, went through her. Gideon was becoming so good at pressing on the bruises closest to her soul and all he had to do was speak the truth.

"Goodbye, Gideon." Without looking at him again, she threw herself into her car and pulled away.

# CHAPTER TWO

THE FERRY WAS gone so Adara couldn't leave the island. She drove through a blur of goat-tracked hills and tree-lined boulevards. Expansive olive branches cast rippling shadows across bobbing heads of yellow and purple wildflowers between scrupulously groomed estates and bleached-white mansions. When she happened upon a lookout, she quickly parked and tried to walk off her trembles.

She'd done it. She'd asked for a divorce.

The word cleaved her in two. She didn't want her marriage to be over. It wasn't just the failure it represented. Gideon was her husband. She wasn't a possessive person. She tried not to get too attached to anything or anyone, but until his affair had come to light, she had believed her claim on him was incontestable. That had meant something to her. She had never been allowed to have anything. Not the job she wanted, not the money in her trust fund, not the family she had briefly had as a child or the one she longed for as an adult.

Gideon was a prize coveted by every woman around her. Being his wife had given her a deep sense of pride, but he'd gone behind her back and even managed to make her writhe with self-blame that it was her fault.

She hadn't made love with him in weeks. It was true. She'd taken care of his needs, though. When he was home. Did he realize he hadn't been home for more than one night at a stretch in months?

Pacing between guilt and virtue, she couldn't escape the position she'd put herself in. Her marriage was over. The marriage she had arranged so her father would stop trying to sell her off to bullies like himself.

Her heart compressed under the weight of remembering how she'd taken such care to ask Gideon for only what seemed reasonable to expect from a marriage: respect and fidelity. That's all. She hadn't asked for love. She barely believed in it, not when her mother still loved the man who had abused her and her children, raising his hand often enough Adara flinched just thinking about it.

No, Adara had been as practical and realistic as she could be—strengths she'd honed razor sharp out of necessity. She had found a man whose wealth was on a level with her father's fortune. She had picked one who exhibited incredible control over his emotions, trying to avoid spending her adult life ducking outbursts and negotiating emotional land mines. She had accommodated Gideon in every way, from the very fair prenup to learning how to please him in bed. She had never asked for romance or signs of affection, not even flowers when she was in hospital recovering from a miscarriage.

Her hand went instinctively to her empty womb. After the first one, she'd tried not to bother him much at all, informing him without involving him, not even telling him about the last one. Her entire being pulsated like an open wound as she recalled the silent weeks of waiting and hoping, then the first stain of blood and the painful, isolated hours that had followed.

While Gideon had been in Barcelona, faithful bitch Lexi at his side.

She had learned nothing from her mother, Adara realized with a spasm in her chest. Being complacent didn't earn you anything but a cheating husband. Her marriage was over and it left a jagged burn in her like a bolt of lightning was stuck inside her, buzzing and shorting and trying to escape.

A new life awaited though, unfurling like a rolled carpet before her. She made herself look at it, standing tall under the challenge, extending her spine to its fullest. She concentrated on hardening her resolve, staring with determination across the vista of scalloped waves to distant islands formed from granite. That's what she was now, alone, but strong and rooted.

She'd look for a new home while she was here, she decided. Greece had always been a place where she'd felt hopeful and happy. Her new life started today. Now.

After discovering his room wasn't ready, Gideon went to the patio restaurant attached to the hotel and ordered a beer. He took care of one piece of pressing business on his mobile before he sat back and brooded on what had happened with Adara.

He had never cheated on her.

But for the last year he had spent more time with his PA than his wife.

Adara had known this would be a brutal year though. They both had. Several large projects were coming online at once. He ought to be in Valparaiso right now, opening his new terminal there. It was the ticking off of another item on their five-year plan, something they had mapped out in the first months of their marriage. That plan was pulling them in different directions, her father's death last year and her mother's sinking health not helping. They were rarely in the same room, let alone the same bed, so to be fair it wasn't strictly her fault they weren't tearing up the sheets.

And there had been Lexi, guarding his time so carefully and keeping him on schedule, mentioning that her latest relationship had fallen apart because she was traveling so much, offering with artless innocence to stay in his suite with him so she could be available at any hour.

She had been offering all right, and perhaps he hadn't outright encouraged or accepted, but he was guilty of keeping his options open. Abstinence, or more specifically, Adara's avoidance of wholehearted lovemaking, had made him restless and dissatisfied. He'd begun thinking Adara wouldn't care if he had an affair. She was getting everything she wanted from this marriage: her position as CEO of her father's hotel chain, a husband who kept all the dates she put in his calendar. The penthouse in Manhattan and by the end of the year, a newly built mansion in the Hamptons.

While he'd ceased getting the primary thing *he* wanted out of their marriage: her.

So he had looked at his alternatives. The fact was, though, as easy as Lexi would be, as physically attractive as she was, he wasn't interested in her. She was too much of an opportunist. She'd obviously read into his "I'll think about it" response enough to imagine she had a claim on him.

That couldn't be what had precipitated Adara running here to Greece and another man, though. The Valparaiso arrangements had only been finalized recently. Adara wasn't that impulsive. She would have been thinking about this for a long time before taking action.

His inner core burned. A scrapper in his youth, Gideon had found other ways to channel his aggression when he'd reinvented himself as a coolheaded executive, but the basic street-life survival skill of fighting to keep what was his had never left him. Every territorial instinct he possessed was aroused by her deceit and the threat it represented to all he'd gained.

The sound of a checked footstep and a barely audible gasp lifted his gaze. He took a hit of sexual energy like he'd swallowed two-hundred-proof whiskey, while Adara lost a few shades of color behind her sunglasses. Because she could read the barely contained fury in him? Or because she was still feeling guilty at being caught out?

She gathered herself to flee, but before she could pivot away, he rose with a menacing scrape of his chair leg on the paving stones. Drawing out the chair off the corner of his table, he kept a steady gaze on her to indicate he would come after her if she chose to run. He wanted to know everything about the man who thought he could steal from him.

So he could quietly destroy him.

"The rooms aren't ready," he told her.

"So they've just informed me again." Adara's mouth firmed to a resistant angle, but she moved forward. If there was one thing he could say about her, it was that she wasn't a coward. She met confrontation with a quiet dignity that disconcerted him every time, somehow making him feel like an executioner of an innocent even though he'd never so much as raised his voice at her.

She'd never given him reason to.

Until today.

With the collected poise he found both admirable and frustrating, she set her purse to the side and lowered herself gracefully into the chair he held. He had learned early that passionate women were scene-makers and he didn't care to draw attention to himself. Adara had been a wallflower with a ton of potential, blooming with subtle brilliance as they had made their mark on the social scene in New York, London and Athens, always keeping things understated.

Which meant she didn't wear short-shorts or low-cut tops, but the way her denim cutoffs clung all the way down her toned thighs and the way the crisp cotton of her loose shirt angled over the thrust of her firm breasts was erotic in its own way.

Unwanted male hunger paced with purpose inside him. How could he still want her? He was furious with her.

Without removing her sunglasses or even looking at him as he took his seat, she opened the menu he'd been given. She didn't put it down until the server arrived, then ordered a souvlaki with salad and a glass of the house white.

"The same," Gideon said dismissively.

"You won't speak Greek even to a native in his own country?" Adara murmured in an askance tone as the man walked away.

"Did I use English? I didn't notice," Gideon lied and sensed her gaze staying on him even though she didn't challenge his assertion. Another thing he could count on with his wife: she never pushed for answers he wouldn't give.

Nevertheless, he found himself waiting for her to speak, willing her almost, which wasn't like him. He liked their quiet meals that didn't beleaguer him with small talk.

He wasn't waiting for, "How's the weather," however. He wanted answers.

Her attention lifted to the greenery forming the canopy above them, providing shade against the persistent sun. Blue pots of pink flowers and feathery palms offered a privacy barrier between their table and the empty one next to them. A colorful mosaic on the exterior wall of the restaurant held her attention for a very long time.

He realized she didn't intend to speak at all.

"Adara," he said with quiet warning.

"Yes?" Her voice was steady and thick with calm reason, but he could see her pulse racing in her throat.

She wasn't comfortable and that was a much-needed satisfaction for him since he was having a hard time keeping his balance. Maybe the comfortable routine of their marriage had grown a bit stale for both of them, but that didn't mean you threw it away and ran off to meet another man. None of this gelled with the woman he'd always seen as ethical, coolheaded and highly averse to risk.

"Tell me why." He ground out the words, resenting the instability of this storm she'd thrown him into and the fact he wasn't weathering it up to his usual standard.

Her mouth pursed in distaste. "From the outset I made it clear that I would rather be divorced than put up with infidelity."

"And yet you sneaked away to have an affair," he charged, angry because he'd been blindsided.

"That's not—" A convulsive flinch contracted her features, half hidden by her bug-eyed glasses, but the flash of great pain was unmistakable before she smoothed her expression and tone, appearing unaffected in a familiar way that he suddenly realized was completely fake.

His fury shorted out into confusion. What else did she hide behind that serene expression of hers?

"I'm not having an affair," she said without inflection.

"No?" Gideon pressed, sitting forward, more disturbed by his stunning insight and her revelation of deep emotion than by her claim. Her anguish lifted a host of unexpected feelings in him. It roused an immediate masculine need in him to shield and protect. Something like concern or threat roiled in him, but not combat-ready threat. Something he wasn't sure how to interpret. Adara was like him, unaffected by life. If something was piercing her shell, it had to be bad and that filled him with apprehensive tension.

"Who did you come to see then?" he prodded, unconsciously bracing.

A slight hesitation, then, with her chin still tucked into her neck, she admitted, "My brother."

His tension bled away in a drain of caustic disappointment. As he fell back in his chair, he laced his Greek endearment with sarcasm. "Nice try, *matia mou.* Your brothers don't earn enough to build a castle like the one we saw today."

Her head came up and her shoulders went back. With the no-nonsense civility he so valued in her, she removed her sunglasses, folded the arms and set them beside her purse before looking him in the eye.

The golden-brown irises were practically a stranger's, he realized with a kick of unease. When was the last time she'd looked right at him? he wondered distantly, while at the same time feeling the tightening inside him that drew on the eye contact as a sexual signal. Like the rest of her, her eyes were understated yet surprisingly attractive when a man took the time to notice. Almond-shaped. Clear. Flecked with sparks of heat.

"I'm referring to my older brother."

Her words left a discordant ring in his ears, dragging him from the dangerous precipice of falling into her eyes.

The server brought their wine. Gideon kept his attention fully focused on Adara's composed expression and contentiously set chin.

"You're the eldest," he stated.

She only lifted her wine to sip while a hollow shadow drifted behind her gaze, giving him a thump of uncertainty, even though he *knew* she only had two brothers, both younger than her twenty-eight years. One was an antisocial accountant who traveled the circuit of their father's hotel chain auditing ledgers, the other a hellion with a taste for big engines and fast women, chasing skirt the way their father had.

Given her father's peccadilloes, he shouldn't be surprised a half sibling had turned up, but older? It didn't make sense and he wasn't ready to let go of his suspicions about an affair.

"How did you find out about him? Was there something in the estate papers after your father passed?"

"I've always known about him." She set aside her wine with a frown of distaste. "I think that's off."

"Always?" Gideon repeated. "You've never mentioned him."

"We don't talk, do we?" Golden orbs came back, charged with electric energy that made him jolt as though she'd touched a cattle prod to his internal organs.

No. They didn't talk. He preferred it that way.

Their server arrived with their meals. Gideon asked for Adara's wine to be changed out. With much bowing and apologies, a fresh glass was produced. Adara tried it and stated it was fine.

As the server walked away, Adara set down her glass with another grimace.

"Still no good?" Gideon tried it. It was fine, perhaps not as dry as she usually liked, but he asked, "Try again?"

"No. I feel foolish that you sent back the first one."

That was so like her to not want to make a fuss, but he considered calling back the waiter all the same. Stating that they didn't talk was an acknowledgment of an elephant. It was the first knock on a door he didn't want opened.

At the same time, he wanted to know more about this supposed brother of hers. Sharing was a two-way street though and hypocrite that he was, he'd prefer backstory to flow only one way. He glanced at the offending wine, ready to seize it as an excuse to keep things inconsequential between them.

And yet, as Adara picked up her fork and hovered it over her rice, she gave him the impression of being utterly without hope. Forlorn. The hairs rose all over his body as he picked up signals of sadness that he'd never caught an inkling of before.

"Do you want to talk about him?" he asked carefully.

She lifted her shoulder. "I've never been allowed to before so I don't suppose one more day of silence matters." It was her conciliatory tone, the one that put everything right and allowed them to move past the slightest hiccup in their marriage.

What marriage? She wanted a divorce, he reminded himself.

Instinct warned him this was dangerous ground, but he also sensed he'd never have another chance to understand if he didn't seize this one. "Who wouldn't let you talk about him?" he asked gruffly.

A swift glance gave him the answer. Her father, of course. He'd been a hard man of strong opinions and ancient views. His daughter could run a household, but her husband would control the hotels. Her share of the family fortune wasn't hers to squander as her brothers might, but left in a trust doled out by tightly worded language, the bulk of the money to be held for her children. The male ones.

Gideon frowned, refusing to let himself be sidetracked by the painful subject of heirs.

"I assume this brother was the product of an affair? Something your father didn't want to be reminded of?"

"He was my mother's indiscretion." Adara frowned at her plate, her voice very soft, her expression disturbingly young and bewildered. "He lived with us until he left for school." She lifted anxious eyes, words pouring out of her in a rush as if she'd held on to them for decades. "My aunt explained years later that my father didn't know at first that Nico wasn't his. When he found out, he had him sent to boarding school. It was awful. That's all they'd tell me, that he'd gone to school. I knew I was starting the next year and I was terrified I'd be forgotten the same way."

A stitch pulled in his chest. His childhood predisposed him to hate the thought of any child frightened by anything. He *felt* her confusion and fear at losing her brother mixed with the terror of not knowing what would happen to herself. It made him nauseous.

Her expression eased into something poignant. "But then we saw him at my aunt's in Katarini over the summer. He was fine. He told me about his school and I couldn't wait to go myself, to be away from the angry man my father had turned into, make new friends..." Her gaze faded to somewhere in the distance. "But I was sent to day school in New York and we saw Nico only a few more times after that. One day I asked if we would see him, and my father—"

Gideon wouldn't have known what she failed to say aloud if he hadn't been watching her so intently, reading her lips because he could barely hear her. Her tongue touched the corner of her mouth where a hairline scar was sometimes visible between her morning shower and her daily application of makeup. She'd told him it had come from a childhood mishap.

A wrecking ball hit him in the middle of his chest. "He hit you?"

Her silence and embarrassed bite of her lip spoke volumes.

His torso felt as if it split open and his teeth clenched so hard he thought they'd crack. His scalp prickled and his blood turned to battery acid.

"I didn't ask again," she said in her quick, sweep-it-under-the-rug way. "I didn't let the boys say his name. I let it go. I learned to let a lot of things go."

Like equal rights. Like bad decisions with the hotel chain that were only now being repaired after her father was dead. Like the fact that her brothers were still boys because they'd been raised by a child: her.

Gideon had seen the dysfunction, the alcoholic mother and the overbearing father, the youngest son who earned his father's criticism, and the older children who hadn't, but received plenty of it anyway. Adara had always managed the volatile dynamics with equanimity, so Gideon hadn't tried to stir up change. If he had suspected physical abuse was the underbelly of it all…

His fist clenched. "You should have told me," he said.

Another slicing glance repeated the obvious. *We don't talk.*

His guts turned to water. No, they didn't and because of that he'd let her down. If there was one thing his wife had never asked of Gideon, but that he'd regarded as his sacred duty, it was his responsibility to protect her. Adara was average height and kept herself toned and in good shape, but she was undeniably female. Her bones were smaller, her muscles not as thick as a man's. She was pre-ordained by nature to be vulnerable to a male's greater strength. Given what had happened to his own mother, he'd lay down his life for any woman, especially one who depended on him.

"At any time since I've known you," he forced himself to ask, "did he—"

"No," she answered bluntly, but her tone was tired. "I learned, Gideon."

It wasn't any sort of comfort.

How had he not seen this? He'd always assumed she was reserved because she had been raised by strict parents. She was ambitious and focused on material gain because most immigrant families to America were. *He* was.

And compliant? Well, it was just her nature.

But no, it was because she had been abused.

He couldn't help staring at her, reeling in disbelief. Not disbelieving she had been mistreated, but that he hadn't known. What else did he not know about her? he wondered uneasily.

Adara forced herself to eat as though nothing was wrong, even though Gideon's X-ray stare made her so nervous she felt as if her bones were developing radiation blisters. Why had she told him? And why did it upset her that he knew what she'd taken such pains to hide from the entire world? She had nothing to be ashamed of. Her father's abuse wasn't her fault.

Sharing her past made her squirm all the same. It was such a dark secret. So close to the heart. Shameful because she had never taken action against her father, trying instead to do everything in her power to keep what remained of her family intact. And she'd been so young.

Her eyebrows were trying to pull into a worried frown. She habitually noted the tension and concentrated on relaxing her facial muscles, hiding her turmoil. Taking a subtle breath, she begged the constriction in her throat to ease.

"He went by his father's name," she told Gideon, taking up the subject of her brother as the less volatile one and using it to distract his intense focus from her. "I found his blogs at one point, but since he had never tried to contact us I didn't know if he'd want to hear from me. I couldn't reach out anyway," she dismissed with a shrug. "Not while my father was alive." She had feared, quite genuinely, that he would kill her. "But as soon as Papa died, I started thinking about coming here."

"But never told me."

She flinched, always sensitive to censure.

Her reaction earned a short sigh.

She wasn't going to state the obvious again though, and it wasn't as if she was laying blame. The fact they didn't talk was as much her fault as his, she knew that. Talking about personal things was difficult for her. She'd grown up in silence, never acknowledging the unpleasant, always avoiding points of conflict so they didn't escalate into physical altercations. Out of self-defense she had turned into a thinker who never revealed what she wanted until she had pondered the best approach and was sure she could get it without raising waves.

"I didn't tell anyone I was coming here, not even my brothers. I didn't want anyone talking me out of it." It was a thin line in the sand. She wouldn't be persuaded to leave until she'd seen her brother. She needed Gideon to recognize that.

He didn't argue and they finished their meals with a thick cloud of tension between them. The bouzouki music from the speakers sounded overly loud as sultry heat layered the hot air into claustrophobic blankets around them.

The minute the server removed their plates, Adara stood and gathered her things, grasping at a chance to draw a full breath. "Thank you for lunch. Goodbye, Gideon."

His hand snaked out to fasten around her wrist.

Her heart gave a thump, his touch always making her pulse leap. She glared at the strong, sun-browned fingers. It wasn't a hard grip. It was warm and familiar and she hated herself for liking it. That gave her the strength to say what she had to.

"Will you contact Halbert or shall I?" She ignored the spear of anguish that pierced her as she mentioned their lawyer's name.

"I fired Lexi."

"Really." She gave her best attempt at blithe lack of interest, but her arteries constricted so each beat of her heart was like a hammer blow inside her.

He shifted his grip ever so slightly, lining up his fingertips on her wrist, no doubt able to feel the way her pulse became ferocious and strong. Not that he gave anything away. His fiercely handsome features were as watchful as a predator's, his eyes hidden behind his mirrored aviators.

"She had no right to speak to you as she did." His assertive tone came across as almost protective. "Implying things that weren't true. I haven't cheated on you, Adara. There's no reason for us to divorce."

As a spasm of agitated panic ran through her, Adara realized she'd grasped Lexi as a timely excuse. Thoughts of divorce had been floating through her mind for weeks, maybe even from the day she had realized she was pregnant again. *If I lose this one, I'll leave him and never have to go through this again.*

"Actually, Gideon," she said with a jagged edge to her hushed voice, "there's no reason for us to stay married. Let me go, please."

# CHAPTER THREE

*No reason to stay married?*

Gideon's head nearly exploded as Adara walked away. How about the luxury cruise ship they were launching next year? The ultimate merger of his shipbuilding corporation and her hotel chain, it wasn't just a crown jewel for both entities, it was a tying together of the two enterprises in a way that wouldn't be easy to untangle. They couldn't divorce at this stage of that project.

Gideon hung back to scratch his name on the bill while tension flooded back into him, returning him to a state of deep aggravation. Neither of them had cheated, but she still wanted a divorce. Why? Did she not believe him?

It was too hot to race after her, and his stride was long enough that he closed in easily as she climbed the road behind the marina shops. Resentment that he was following her at all filled him with gall. He was not a man who chased after women begging for another chance. He didn't have to.

But the fact that Adara saw no reason to continue their marriage gave him a deep sense of ignorance. They had ample financial reasons. What else did she want from the union? More communication? Fine, they could start talking.

Even as he considered it, however, resistance rose in him. And at that exact moment, as he'd almost caught up to Adara, the stench of rotting garbage came up off a restaurant Dumpster, carried on a breeze flavored with the dank smells of the marina: tidal flats, diesel exhaust and fried foods. It put him squarely back in his childhood, searching for a safe place to sleep while his mother worked the docks in Athens.

Adara didn't even know who she was married to. Divorce would mean court papers, identification, paparazzi... Marrying under an assumed name had been tricky enough and he lived a much higher profile now. He couldn't risk divorce. But if he wasn't legally married to her, did he have a right to keep her tied to him?

His clothes began to feel tight. "Adara, you'll get sunstroke. Come back to the hotel," he ordered.

She seemed to flinch at the sound of his voice. Pausing, she turned to face him, her defensive tension obvious in her stiff posture.

"Gideon—" She seemed to search for words around her feet, or perhaps she was looking for stones to scare him away. "Look, I've taken this time as vacation." She flicked her thick plait back over her shoulder. "The gardener said my brother will be back in a few days. I'm staying until I meet him. In the meantime, I might as well see the sights. There's a historical viewpoint up here. You can go back to New York or on to Valparaiso as scheduled. Legal can work out the details. I'm not going to contest anything. Neither of us will be bothered by any of this."

Not bothered? He *wished*. He was shaken to the bone by what she'd revealed, not the least bit comfortable with the fact he'd been so oblivious. It gave him new eyes on her and them and yes, he could see that they'd foundered a bit, but this wasn't so bad you abandoned ship and let it sink.

Apparently Adara was prepared to, offering up one of her patented sweep, fold, tuck maneuvers that tidied away all conflicts. *Mama's ask-*

*ing about Christmas. We can take two cars if you like, so you can stay in the city?*

Her accommodating nature was suddenly irritating in the extreme, partly because he knew he *should* get back to work rather than standing here in the middle of the road in the middle of the Mediterranean watching her walk away. She might have lightened her workload in anticipation of coming here, but he hadn't. Myriad to-dos ballooned in his mind while ahead of him Adara's pert backside sashayed up the incline of the deserted street.

He wasn't stupid enough to court heat exhaustion to keep a woman, but the reality was only a very dense man would let that beautiful asset walk away from him without at least trying to coax her to stay. Admiring her round butt, he recollected it was the first thing he'd noticed about her before she'd turned around with an expression of cool composure that had assured him she was all calm water and consistent breeze.

The rest of the pieces had fallen into place like predetermined magic. Their dealings with each other had been simple and straightforward. Adara was untainted by the volatile emotions other women were prone to. Perhaps the smooth sailing of their marriage was something he'd taken for granted, but she must know that he valued it and her.

Or did she? He was about as good at expressing his feelings as he was at arranging flowers.

Disquiet nudged at him as he contemplated how to convince her to continue their marriage. He knew how to physically seduce a woman, but emotional persuasion was beyond his knowledge base.

Why in hell couldn't they just go back to the way things had been?

Not fully understanding why he did it, he caught up to her at the viewpoint. It was little more than a crosspiece of weathered wood in dry, trampled grass. A sign in English identified it as a spot from which ships had been sighted during an ancient war. It also warned about legal action should tourists attempt to climb down to the beach below. A sign in Greek cautioned the locals to swim at their own risk.

Adara shaded her eyes, but he had the sense she was shielding herself from him as much as the sun. Her breasts rose and fell with exertion and her face glowed with light perspiration, but also with mild impatience. She didn't really give a damn about old ships and history, did she? This was just an excuse to get away from him.

He experienced a pinch of compunction that he'd never bothered to find out *what* she gave a damn about. She was quiet. He liked that about her, but it bothered him that he couldn't tell what she was thinking right now. If he didn't know what she was thinking, how would he talk her round to *his* way of thinking?

Her beauty always distracted him. That was the truth of it. She was oddly youthful today with her face clean of makeup and her hair in pigtails like a schoolgirl, but dressed down or to the nines, she always stirred a twist of possessive desire in his groin.

*That* was why he didn't want a divorce.

His clamoring libido was a weakness that governed him where she was concerned. The sex had always been good, but not exactly a place where they met as equals. In the beginning he'd been favored with more experience. The leader. He wasn't hampered by shyness or other emotions that women attached to intimacy. He'd tutored her and loved it.

Adara had maintained a certain reserve in the bedroom that she had never completely allowed to let slide away, however. While the sex had always been intense and satisfying, the power had subtly shifted over time into her favor. She decided when and how much and *if.*

Resentment churned in him, bringing on a scowl. He didn't like that she was threatening him on so many levels. Yanking the rug on sex was bad enough. Now all that he'd built was on a shaky foundation.

*Why?* Did it have to do with her fear of her father? Did she fear him? Blame him? Apprehension kept him from asking.

And Adara gave no clue to her thoughts, acting preoccupied with reading the signage, ignoring him, aggravating him further.

She peered over the edge of the steep slope to where a rope was tied to the base of the wooden crosspiece and, without a word, looped the thin strap of her purse over her head and shoulder then maneuvered to the edge of the cliff. Taking up the rope, she clung to it as she began a very steep, backward descent.

Gideon was taken aback. "What the hell are you doing?"

She paused. Uncertainty made her bottom lip flinch before she firmed it. "Going swimming."

"Like hell you are." Who *was* this woman?

The anxiety that spasmed across her features transitioned through uncertainty before being overcome by quiet defiance. "I always did as I was told because I was scared my father would punish me. Unless you intend to take up controlling my behavior with violence, I'm doing what I want from now on."

The pit of his belly was still a hard knot over her revelations about her childhood. He would never hurt her or threaten to and was now even more inclined to treat her with kid gloves. At the same time, everything in him clamored to exert control over her, get what he wanted and put an end to this nonsense. The conflicting feelings, too deep for comfort, left him standing there voicelessly glaring his frustration.

Despite her bold dare, there was something incredibly vulnerable in her stance of toughness though. An air of quiet desperation surrounded her as tangibly as the hardened determination she was trying to project.

She wanted to prove something. He didn't know what it was, but bullying her into going back to the hotel wasn't the way to find out. It wouldn't earn him any points toward keeping their marriage intact either.

"It's fine, Gideon. You can go," she said in her self-possessed way. *Papa doesn't think the Paris upgrade is necessary. I'll find my own way home after our meeting.*

"And leave you to break your neck? No," he said gruffly.

The way she angled a look up at him seemed to indicate suspicion. Maybe it was deserved. He was chivalrous, always picked up her heavy bags, but neither of them were demonstrative. Maybe he'd never acted so protective before, but she'd never tried to do anything so perilous.

"I won't break my neck," she dismissed and craned it to watch as she tentatively sought a step backward.

A completely foreign clench of terror squeezed his lungs. Did she not see how dangerous this was? He skimmed his hand over his sweat-damp-ened hair.

"Adara, I won't hurt you, but I will get physical if you don't stop right there and at least let me get behind you so I can catch you if you slip."

She stared, mouth pursing in mutiny. "I don't have to ask your permission to live my life, Gideon." *Not anymore*, was the silent punctuation to that.

"Well, I won't ask your permission to save it. Stay put until I get behind you."

He sensed her wariness as he took his time in-specting the rope, approving its marine grade, not-ing it was fairly new and in good repair, as was the upright it was tied to. Assured they weren't going to plunge to their deaths, he let his loose grip slide along the rope until his hand met Adara's.

She stiffened as he brushed past her, making him clench his teeth. When had his touch become toxic?

*Ask*, he chided himself, but things were dis-cordant enough. His assumptions about her were turned on their heads, her predictability com-pletely blown out of the water. He didn't know what to say or what to expect next, so he picked his way down the slope in grim silence, arriving safely on to the pocket of sand between monolithic gray boulders.

The tide was receding, but the cove was steep enough it was still a short beach into a deep pool. It was the type of place young lovers would tryst, and his mind immediately turned that way. Adara wasn't even looking at him, though.

Adara shrugged against the sting of sweat and the disturbing persistence Gideon was showing. She thought they had an unspoken agreement to back off when things got personal, but even though she'd spilled way more of her family history than she'd ever meant to, he was sticking like humidity.

She didn't know how to react to that. And should she thank him for his uncharacteristic show of consideration in accompanying her down here? Or tell him again to shove off? He was so hard to be around sometimes, so unsettling. He was shorting out a brain that was already melting in the heat. She desperately wanted to cool off so she could think straight again, but she hadn't brought a bathing suit and—

Oh, to heck with it. She kicked off her flip-flops and began unbuttoning her shirt.

"Really?" he said, not hiding the startled uptick in his tone.

She didn't let herself waver. Maybe this was out of character, but this was her new life. She was tossing off fear of reprisal, embracing the freedom to follow impulse.

"I miss Greece. My aunt let us run wild here. In Katarini, not this island, but we'd do exactly this: tramp along the beach until we got hot then we'd strip to our underthings and jump in."

"Your aunt was a nudist?" he surmised.

"A free spirit. She never married, never had children—" Here Adara faltered briefly. "I intend to emulate her from now on."

She shed her shorts and ran into the water in her bra and panties, feeling terribly exposed as she left her decision to never have children evaporating on the sizzling sand.

The clear, cool water rose to her waist within a few splashing steps. She fell forward and ducked under, arrowing deep into the silken blur filled with the muted cacophony of creaks and taps and swishing currents.

When her lungs were ready to burst, she shot up for air, blinking the water from her eyes and licking the salt from her lips, baptized into a new version of herself. The campy phrase *the first day of the rest of your life* came to her with a pang of wistful anticipation.

Gideon's head appeared beside her, his broad shoulders flexing as he splayed out his arms to keep himself afloat. His dark lashes were matted and glinting, his thick hair sleeked back off his face, exposing his angular bone structure and taking her breath with his action-star handsomeness. The relief of being in the cool water relaxed his expression, while his innate confidence around the water—in any situation, really—made him incredibly compelling.

She would miss that sense of reliability, she acknowledged with a hitch of loss.

"I've never tried to curb your independence," he asserted. "Marrying me gained you your freedom."

They'd never spoken so bluntly about her motives. She'd only stated in the beginning that she'd like to keep working until they had a family, but he knew her better after her confession today. He was looking at her as though he could see right into her.

It made her uncomfortable.

"Marrying at all was a gamble," she acknowledged with a tentative honesty that caused her veins to sting with apprehension. "But you're right. I was fairly sure I'd have more control over my life living with you than I had with my father."

She squinted against the glare off the water as she silently acknowledged that she'd learned to use Gideon to some extent, pitting him against her father when she wanted something for herself. Not often and not aggressively, just with a quiet comment that *Gideon* would prefer this or that.

"You had women working for you in high-level positions," she noted, remembering all the minute details that had added up to a risk worth taking. "You were shocked that I didn't know how to drive. You fired that man who was harassing your receptionist. I was reasonably certain my life with you would be better than it was with my father so I took a chance." She glanced at him, wondering if he judged her harshly for advancing her interests through him.

"So what's changed?" he challenged. "I taught you to drive. I put you in charge of the hotels. Do you want more responsibility? Less? Tell me. I'm not trying to hem you in."

No, Gideon wasn't a tyrant. He was ever so reasonable. She'd always liked that about him, but today that quality put her on edge. "Lexi—"

"—is a nonissue," he stated curtly. "Nothing happened and do you know why? Because I thought *you* were having an affair and got myself on a plane and chased you down. I didn't even think twice about it. Why didn't *you* do that? Why didn't you confront me? Why didn't you ask me why I'd even consider letting another woman throw herself under me?"

"You don't have to be so crude about it!" She instinctively propelled herself backward, pushing space between herself and the unbearable thought of him sleeping with another woman. She hadn't been able to face it herself, let along confront him, not with everything else that had happened.

"You said we don't talk," he said with pointed aggression. "Let's. You left me twisting with sexual frustration. Having an affair started to look like a viable option. If you didn't want me going elsewhere, why weren't you meeting my needs at home?"

"I did! I—"

"Going down isn't good enough, Adara."

His vulgarity was bad enough, but it almost sounded like a critique and she resented that. She tried hard to please him and could tell that he liked what she did, so why did he have to be so disparaging about it?

Unbearably hurt, she kicked toward shore, barely turning her head to defend, "I was pregnant. What else could I do?"

How he reacted to that news she didn't care. She just wanted to be away from him, but as her toes found cold, thick sand, she halted. Leaving the water suddenly seemed a horribly exposing thing to do. How stupid to think she could become a new person by shedding a few stitches of clothing. She was the same old worthless Adara who couldn't even keep a baby in her womb.

The sun seared across her shoulders. Her wet hair hung in her eyes and she kept her arms folded tightly across her chest, trying to hold in the agony.

She felt ridiculous, climbing down to this silly beach that was impossible to leave, revealing things that were intensely personal to her and wouldn't matter at all to him.

"What did you say?" He was too close. She flinched, feeling the sharpness of his voice like the tip of a flicking whip.

"You heard me," she managed to say even though her throat was clogging. She clenched her eyes shut, silently begging him to do what he always did. Say nothing and give her space. She didn't want to do this. She never, ever wanted to do this again.

"You *were* pregnant?" His voice moved in front of her.

She turned her head to the side, hating him for cutting off her escape to the beach, hating herself for lacking the courage to take it when she'd had the chance.

Keeping her eyes tightly closed, she dug her fingers into her arms, her whole body aching with tension. "It doesn't matter," she insisted through her teeth. "It's over and I just want a divorce."

Gideon was distantly aware of the sea trying to pull him out with the tide. His entire being was numb enough that he had to concentrate on keeping his feet rooted as he stared at Adara. She was a knot of torment. For the first time he could see her suffering and it made his heart clench. When had she started to care about the miscarriages? The last one had been called into him from across the globe, his offer to come home dismissed as unnecessary.

"Tell me—"

"What is there to tell, Gideon?" Her eyes opening into pits of hopeless fury. Her face creased with sharp lines of grief. "It was the same as every other one. I did the test and held my breath, terrified to so much as bump my hip on the edge of my desk. And just when I let myself believe this time might be different, the backache started and the spotting appeared and then it was twenty-four hours of medieval torture until I was spat out in hell with nothing to show for it. At least I didn't have the humiliation of being assaulted by the people in white coats this time."

She took a step to the side, thinking to circle him and leave the water, but he shifted into her path, his hand reaching to stop her. His expression was appalled. "What do you mean about being assaulted?"

She cringed from his touch, her recoil like a knee into his belly. Gideon clenched his abdominal muscles and curled his fingers into his palm, forcing his hand to his side under the water even though he wanted to grip her with all his strength and squeeze the answers out of her. She couldn't possibly be saying what he thought she was saying.

"What people in white coats?" he demanded, but the words sounded far away. "Are you telling me you didn't go to the hospital?" Intense, fearful dread hollowed out his chest as he watched her mask fear and compunction with a defiant thrust of her chin.

"Do you know what they do to you after you've had a miscarriage? No, you don't. But I do and I'm sick of it. So, no, I didn't go," she declared with bitter rebelliousness.

Horror washed through him in freezing waves.

"We need to get you to a doctor." He flew his gaze to the cliff, terror tightening in him. What the hell had he been thinking, letting her descend to this impossible place?

"It was three weeks ago, Gideon. If it was going to kill me, it would have by now."

"It could have," he retorted, helplessness making him brutal. "You could have bled to death."

She shrugged that off with false bravado, eyes

glossy and red. "At the time that looked like a—what's the expression you used? A viable option?"

It was a vicious slap that he deserved. While he'd been contemplating an affair, she'd been losing the battle to keep their baby. Again. And she'd been filled with such dejection she'd refused medical care and courted death.

The fact she'd let herself brush elbows with the Grim Reaper made him so agitated, he clipped out a string of foul Greek curses. "Don't talk like that. Damn it, you should have told me."

"Why?" she lashed out in uncharacteristic confrontation. "Do you think I enjoy telling you what a failure I am? It's not like you care. You just go back to work while I sit there screaming inside." She struck a fist onto the surface of the water. "I hate it. I can't go on like this. I won't. *I want a divorce.*"

She splashed clumsily from the surf, her wet underpants see-through, her staggered steps so uncoordinated and indicative of her distress it made him want to reach out for her, but he was rooted in the water, aghast.

He cared. Maybe he'd never told her, but each lost baby had scored his heart. This one, knowing he could have walked into the penthouse and found both of them dead, lanced him with such deep horror he could barely acknowledge it.

*She* was the one who had appeared not to care. The fact she'd been so distraught she hadn't sought medical attention told him how far past the end of her rope she had been, but she'd never let him see any of that.

He followed her on heavy feet, pausing where they'd left their clothes.

She gave him a stark look, her gaze filling with apprehension as she took in that he was completely naked. Her fingers hurried to button her blouse.

Hell. He wasn't trying to come on to her.

"Adara." A throb of tender empathy caught in him like a barbed hook. He reached out to cup her neck, her hair a weight on his wrist.

She stiffened, but he didn't let her pull away. He carefully took her shoulder in his opposite hand and made her face him, for once driven by a need deeper than sexual to touch her.

"I'm sorry," he said with deep sincerity. "Sorry we lost another baby, sorry you felt you couldn't tell me. I do care. You've always been stoic about it and I've followed your lead. How could I know it was devastating you like this if you didn't say?"

She shivered despite the heat. Her blink released a single tear from the corner of her eye. Her plump mouth trembled with vulnerability, and a need to comfort overwhelmed him.

Gideon gathered her in. She seemed so delicate and breakable. He touched his mouth to hers, wanting to reassure, to console.

It wasn't meant to be a pass, but she felt so good. The kiss was a soft press of a juicy fruit to the mouth of a starved man. He couldn't help opening his lips on hers, sliding his tongue along the seam then pressing in for a deep lick of her personal flavor. Involuntarily, his arms tightened while greed swelled in him. Everything in him expanded in one hard kick. His erection pulled to attention in a rush of heat, fed by the erotically familiar scent of his wife.

The feathery touch of her hands whispered from his ribs to his shoulder blades. A needy sob emanated from her throat, encouraging him.

*Here. Now.* His brain shorted into the most basic thoughts as his carnal instincts took over. He skimmed his hand to the wet underpants covering her backside, starting to slide them down even as he deepened the kiss and began to ease them both to the sand.

Adara's knees softened for one heartbeat, almost succumbing, then she broke away from their kiss with a ragged moan, stumbling backward a few steps as she shoved from him with near violence. Her flush of arousal dissolved into a bewildered glare of accusation and betrayal.

That wounded look bludgeoned him like a club.

Without speaking, face white, she gathered her things and moved to the bottom of the rope where she tried to force her wet legs into her denim shorts.

Gideon pinched the bridge of his nose, ears rushing with the blood still pumping hotly through his system, deeply aware that the distance had been closed until he'd forgotten that he was trying to comfort, not seduce. But the sexual attraction between them was something he couldn't help. He wished he could. The fact that he couldn't entirely control his hunger for her bothered him no end.

His thoughts were dark as they returned to the hotel, a fresh sweat on his salted skin as they came through the front doors, with not a word exchanged since the beach. The life he'd created with Adara, so easy on the surface, had grown choppy, teaming with undercurrents. She'd stirred up more emotion in him with this bolt to Greece than he'd suffered in years and he didn't like it.

Part of him wanted to cut and run, but it was impossible now he understood what was driving her request for a divorce: grief. He understood that frame of mind better than she would suspect. He'd even bolted across the ocean in the very same way, more than once, but he was able to think more clearly this time. Losing the baby was heartrending, but he wasn't left alone. He still had her. They needed to stick together. With careful navigation, they'd be back on course and sailing smoothly. When she came out the other side, she'd appreciate that he hadn't let her do anything rash.

He hoped.

Adara blinked as they entered the artificial light of the hotel foyer. The temperature change hit her between the eyes like a blow. The boutique accommodation was the best the island offered, but nothing like the luxury service she took for granted in her thousand-room high-rise hotels. Still, she liked the coziness of this small, out-of-the-way place. She'd give serious thought to developing some hideaways like this herself, she decided.

Another time. Right now she felt like one giant blister, hot and raw, skin so thin she could be nicked open by the tiniest harsh word.

Desire had almost overwhelmed her on the beach. Gideon's kiss had been an oasis in a desert of too many empty days and untouched nights. His heartfelt words, the way he'd enfolded her as if he could make the whole world right again, had filled her with hope and relief. For a few seconds she had felt cherished, even when his kiss had turned from tenderness to hunger. It had all been balm to her injured soul, right up until he'd begun to tilt them to the sand.

Then fear of pregnancy had undercut her arousal. Her next instinct had been to at least give him pleasure. She *liked* making him lose control, but then she'd remembered *it wasn't good enough.*

It had all crashed into her as a busload of confusing emotions: shattered confidence, anger at her own weakness and a sense of being tricked and teased with a promise that would be broken. If she had had other men, perhaps she wouldn't be so susceptible to him, but she was a neophyte where men were concerned, even after five years of marriage. She needed distance from him, to get her head straightened out and her heart put back together.

Gideon was given a room card at the same time she was.

As they departed the front desk for the elevators, she said in a ferocious undertone, "You did not get yourself added to my room." They might share a suite, but never a room. She would *die*.

"I booked my own," he said stiffly, the reserve in his voice making her feel as if she'd done something wrong. She hadn't! Had she? Should she have been more open about the miscarriages?

She shook off guilt she didn't want to feel. "Gideon—" she began to protest.

"What? You're allowed a vacation, but I'm not?"

She tilted her head in disgruntlement. That was not what she was driving at. She wanted distance from him.

"Would you like to eat here tonight or try somewhere else?" he said in a continuation of assumptions that were making her crazy.

"It's been a lot of travel getting here and already a long day. I'm going to shower and rest, possibly sleep through dinner," she asserted, silently thinking, *Go away.* Her feelings toward him were infinitely easier to bear when half a globe separated them.

"I'll email you when I get hungry then. If you're up, you can join me. If not, I won't disturb you."

She eyed him, suspicious of yet another display of ultraconsideration, especially when he walked her to her room. At the last second, he turned to insert his card in the door across from hers.

Her heart gave a nervous jump. So close. Immediately, a jangle went through her system, eagerness and fretfulness tying her into knots. She locked herself into her room, worried that he'd badger her into spending time with him that would roll into rolling around with him. She couldn't do it. She didn't have it in her to risk pregnancy and go through another miscarriage.

Even though she ached rather desperately to feel his strong, naked body moving over and into hers.

Craving and humiliation tormented her through her shower and stayed with her when she crawled into bed. She wanted him so much. It made her bury her head under her pillow. She couldn't live with a man she had no defenses against.

Steadfast to his word, Gideon didn't disturb her. Adara woke to fading light beyond her closed curtains, startled she'd fallen asleep at all, head fuzzy from a hard four-hour nap.

Like an adolescent desperate for a hint of being popular, she checked her email before rising from bed, scrolling past the work ones that were piling up and honing in on Gideon's.

Brief and veiled as all his communications tended to be, the message was nevertheless maddeningly effective at driving her into fresh clothes and across the hall.

Your brother called. Dinner?

# CHAPTER FOUR

ADARA WAS SO anxious, she blurted out her questions before Gideon fully opened his door. "What did he say? Is he coming here?"

The swipe of her tongue over her dry lips, however, was more to do with Gideon's bare chest beneath the open buttons of his white shirt than nerves at the thought of seeing her brother. Why had he brought those wretched jeans that were more white than blue, so old they clung to his hips and thighs like a second skin? No shoes either, she noted. The man was so unconsciously sexy she couldn't handle it. She'd never known how to handle it.

It didn't help that he looked at her like he could see into the depths of her soul. All that she'd told him today, the way he'd reacted, rushed back to strip her defenses down to the bare minimum.

"He won't be back to the island for a couple of days," he said, holding his door wider. "I had a table set on my balcony. They have our order, I only need to call down to let them know we're ready for it."

Adara folded her arms across the bodice of her crinkled white sundress, grossly uncomfortable as she watched him move to the hotel phone, his buttocks positively seductive in that devoted denim.

"I'd rather go down to the restaurant," she said, stomach fluttering as she struggled to assert herself.

"It's booked. And we can talk more privately here." He projected equanimity, but he sent her an assessing glance that warned her he wasn't one hundred percent pleased by this new argumentative Adara.

She swallowed, not at ease in this skin either, but she couldn't go on the old way. At the same time, she couldn't help wondering what had transpired in his conversation with her brother that they needed privacy. Nico lived here on the island, she reminded herself. It wouldn't be fair to bandy about his private business in public.

Out of consideration to him, she stepped cautiously into Gideon's room. The layout was a mirror of her executive room with a king-size bed, lounge area and workstation. Gideon had a better view, but she had taken what they had offered, not asking for upgrades. He, on the other hand, demanded the best.

Moving into the velvety night air of his balcony, she listened to him finalize their dinner then come up behind her to pour two glasses of wine. The sunset turned the golden liquid pink as he offered her a glass.

"To improved communication," he said, touching the rim of his glass to hers.

Adara couldn't resist a facetious "Really? And how long do you intend to make me wait to hear all that you and my brother said to each other?"

"I'll tell you now and you can leave before the meals arrive, if you're going to be so suspicious." He sounded insulted.

Adara pressed the curve of her glass to her flat mouth, a tiny bit ashamed of herself. She lowered the glass without wetting her lips. "You can't deny you used his call like some kind of bait-and-switch technique."

"Only because I genuinely want to salvage this marriage. We can't do that if we don't see each other." The sincerity in his gaze made her heart trip with an unsteady thump.

Why would he want to stay married? She was giving up on children. They both had enough money of their own without needing any of each other's. She tilted her glass, sipping the chilled wine that rolled across her tongue in a tart, cool wave that… *Bleh.* An acrid stain coated her mouth.

*Stress*, she thought. Rather than being someone who drank her troubles away, she avoided alcohol when she was keyed up. The way her mother had drowned in booze, and the cruelty it had brought out in her father, had always kept Adara cautious of the stuff. Her body was telling her this was one of those times she should leave it alone.

Setting her glass on the table, she leaned her elbows on the balcony railing and said, "Would you please tell me what happened with Nico?"

"He called asking for us. The front desk tried my room first and I told him you were resting."

"How did he even know we were here?" she asked with surprise.

"Ah. Now, *that's* amusing." He didn't sound amused. He turned his back on the sunset and his cheeks hollowed as he contemplated some scowl-inducing inner thought. "I assumed he had a crack security team, but he has something far more sophisticated—an island grapevine. You didn't tell the gardener you were related to him, so a strange woman asking about him set off speculation, enough that he got a call from a well-meaning neighbor and logged in to his gate camera. He recognized you and I guess he's kept tabs on you over the years, too, because he knew your married name. The island only has four hotels, so it was quick work to track us to this one. He invited us to stay at his villa until he gets home."

"Really?" Adara rotated to Gideon like a flower to the sun, buoyed by what Nico's interest and invitation represented. *He wanted to see her.*

A thought occurred, making her clench her hand on the railing. Gideon was a very private person who kept himself removed from all but the most formal of social contact. He wouldn't want to stay in a stranger's house full of unfamiliar staff.

An excruciating pang of loss ambushed her. She would have to continue her journey alone, her request for independence and divorce granted even as her husband's desire for reconciliation hung in the air. As cavalier as she wanted to be about leaving him, it wasn't painless or easy. Her heart started to shrivel as she looked to the emptiness that was her future.

"I told him I would leave it up to you to decide," Gideon continued. "But that I expected we'd move over there tomorrow because you're eager to renew ties." He took another healthy draw from his wine.

Adara blinked, shocked that Gideon would make such a concession. It made everything he said about salvaging their marriage earnest and powerful.

"You said that?" She reached out instinctively, setting her free hand on his sleeve so he would look at her, then feeling awkward when he only stared at her narrow hand on his tense forearm. She pulled her hand away. "I didn't expect you to understand."

"I'm not an idiot. I've got the message that there's more going on than you've let me see." Now his gaze came up and his dark-chocolate irises were intensely black in the fading light. "I want you to quit keeping so much to yourself, Adara."

Longing speared into her, but so did fear. The

words *I can't* lodged in her throat. She never shared, never asked for help. She didn't know how.

A knock at the door heralded room service. Gideon moved to let the server in and stood back as the meals were set out. Gideon's knowledge of her tastes and his desire to please were well at the forefront. He'd ordered prawn soup, fried calamari, and baked fish fillets on rice with eggplant. Delicious scents of scorched ouzo and tangy mint made her mouth water. Their climb to the beach, coupled with the time change, had her stomach trying to eat itself. Much as she knew it would be better not to encourage either of them that their marriage had a chance, she couldn't help sinking into the chair he held.

Winking lights bobbed on the water, live music drifted from the restaurant below and the warm evening air stroked her skin with a sensual breeze. The server closed the door on his way out and the big bed stood with inviting significance just inside the room.

And then there was the man, still barefoot, still with his shirt hanging open off his shoulders, the pattern of hair across his chest and abdomen accentuating his firm pecs and six-pack stomach.

How he managed casual elegance with such a disreputable outfit, she didn't know, but the woman in her not only responded, but melted into a puddle of sexual craving.

She was in very real danger of being seduced by nothing more than his presence.

Frightened of herself, she stole a furtive glance into his face and found him watching her closely, not smug, but his gaze was sharp with awareness that she was reacting to him. Her cheeks heated with embarrassment at not being able to help this interminable attraction to him.

Gideon couldn't remember ever being so tuned to a woman, not out of bed anyway, and even at that he and Adara had fallen into certain patterns. Now that he was beginning to see how much she disguised behind a placid expression or level tone, he was determined to pick up every cue. The fact he'd just caught her lusting after him in her reserved way pleased him intensely, but her reluctance to let nature take its course confused him.

"I've been faithful to you, Adara. I hope you believe that."

She stopped chewing for a thoughtful moment.

Her brows came together in a frown he couldn't interpret. Worry? Misery? Defeat?

"I do," she finally said, but her tone seemed to qualify the statement.

"But?" he prompted.

"It doesn't change the fact that one of the major reasons we married…" Her brows pulled again and this time it was pure pain, like something deeply embedded was being wrenched out of her.

He tensed, knowing what was coming and not liking the way it penetrated his walls either.

"Obviously I'm not able to give you children," she said with strained composure. "I won't even try. Not anymore."

The bitter acceptance he read beneath her mask of self-possession, her trounced distress, was so tangible, he reached across to cover her shaking hand where she gripped her knife. Her knuckles felt sharp as barnacles where they poked against his palm.

He would give anything to spare her this anguish.

"Having children was a condition that came from your side of the table. It's not a deal-breaker for me," he reassured her.

If anything, she grew more distraught. "You never wanted children?"

*Tread lightly,* he cautioned himself, touching a thoughtful tongue to his bottom lip. "It's not that I never wanted them. If that were true, I'd be a real monster for putting you through all you've suffered in trying to have one. I'm very—" *Disappointed* wasn't a strong enough word.

"I'm sad," he admitted, drawing his hand back as he took the uncharacteristic step of admitting to feelings. He'd been powerless at sea in a storm once and hadn't felt as helpless and vulnerable as he had each time she'd miscarried. This one he'd learned about today was the worst yet, filling him with visions of coming upon her dead. It was too horrifying a thing to happen to a person even once in a lifetime and he'd been through it twice already. He couldn't stomach thinking of finding her lifeless and white.

Then there was the bereft sense of loss that he'd known nothing about the baby before it was gone. He hated having no control over the situation, hated being unable to give her something she wanted that seemed as if it should be so simple. He hated how the whole thing stirred up old grief. He ought to be over forming deep attachments. He'd certainly fought against developing any. But he wished he'd known those babies and felt cheated that he hadn't been given the chance.

He swiped his clammy palm down his thigh.

"I'm sad, too," she whispered thickly, gaze fixed on her sweating glass of ice water. "I wanted a family. A real one, not a broken one like I had."

"So, it wasn't just pressure from your father to give him the heir your brothers weren't providing?"

She made a motion of negation, mouth pouted into sorrow.

*Damn,* he swore silently, thinking his version of her as merely ticking *children* off the list with everything else would have been so much easier to navigate.

"I thought you were like my father, not really wanting a family, but determined to have an heir. A boy." *Of course,* her tiny shrug added silently.

He could see wary shadows in her eyes as she confessed what had been in her mind. She wasn't any more comfortable with being honest than he was. He sure as hell didn't enjoy hearing her unflattering assessment of his attitude toward progeny.

"I wasn't taking it that lightly," he said, voice so tight she tensed. "But I didn't know how much it meant to you."

Any other time in his life he would have swiftly put an end to such a deeply personal conversation, but right now, unpleasant as it was, he had to allow Adara to see she wasn't the only one hurt by this. She wasn't the only one with misconceptions.

"I never knew my father, so that gave me certain reservations about what kind of parent I'd make. You're not anything like my mother, which is a very good thing in most ways, but she did have a strong maternal instinct. I never saw you take an interest in other people's children. Your family isn't the warmest. Frankly, I expected you to schedule a C-section, hire a nanny and mark that task 'done.'"

He'd seen this look on Adara's face before, after a particularly offside, cutting remark from her father. Her lashes swept down, her brow tensed and her nostrils pinched ever so slightly with a slow, indrawn breath. He'd always assumed she was gathering her patience, but today he saw it differently. She was absorbing a blow.

One that he had delivered. His heart clutched in his chest. *Don't put me in the same category as that man.*

"I'm just telling you how it looked, Adara." His voice was gruff enough to make her flinch.

"Like you're some kind of open book, letting me see your thoughts and feelings?" She pushed her plate away with hands that trembled. "I've told you more about myself today than I've ever shared with anyone and all I've heard back is that you're sad I miscarried. Well, I should damn well hope so! They were your babies too."

She rose and tried to escape, but he was faster, his haste sending his chair tumbling with a clatter, his hands too rough on her when he pulled her to stand in front of him, but her challenge made him slip the leash on his control.

"What do you want me to say? That I hadn't believed in God for years, but when I took you to the hospital that first time, I gave praying a shot and felt completely betrayed when He took that baby anyway? That I got drunk so I wouldn't cry? *Every time.* Damn it, I haven't been able to close my eyes since the beach without imagining walking into your bathroom and finding you dead in a pool of blood." He gave her a little shake. "Is that the kind of sharing you need to hear?"

Her shattered gaze was more than he could bear, the searching light in them pouring over his very soul, picking out every flaw and secret he hid from the rest of the world. It was painful in the extreme and even though he would never want to inflict more suffering on her, he was relieved when she crumpled with anguish and buried her face in her hands.

He pulled her into his chest, the feel of her fragile curves a pleasure-pain sting. She stiffened as he pinned her to him, but he only dug his fingers into her loose hair, massaging her scalp and pressing his lips to her crown, forcing the embrace because he needed it as much as she did.

"It's okay, I'm not going to mess it up this time." His body was reacting to her scent and softness, always did, but he ignored it and hoped she would too. "I'm sorry we keep losing babies, Adara. I'm sorry I didn't let you see it affects me."

"I can't try anymore, Gideon." Her voice was small and thick with finality, buried in his chest.

"I know." He rubbed his chin on the silk of her hair, distantly aware how odd this was to hold her like this, not as a prelude to sex, not because they were dancing, but to reassure her. "I don't expect you to try. That's what I'm saying. We don't have to divorce over this. We can stay married."

She lifted her face, her expression devastated beyond tears, and murmured a baffled "I don't even know why you want to."

Under her searching gaze, his inner defenses instinctively locked into place. Practicalities and hard facts leaped to his lips, covering up deeper, less understood motivations. "We're five years into merging our fortunes," he pointed out.

Adara dropped her chin and gathered herself, pressing for freedom.

His answer hadn't been good enough.

His muscles flexed, reluctant to let her go, but he had to. *Feelings,* he thought, and scowled with displeasure. What was she looking for? A declaration of love? That had never been part of their bargain and it wasn't a step he was willing to take. Losing babies he hadn't known was bad enough. Caring deeply for Adara would make him too vulnerable.

He reached to right his chair, nodding at her seat

when she only watched him. "Sit down, let's keep talking about this."

"What's the point?" she asked despairingly.

The coward in him wanted to agree and let this madness blow away like dead ashes from a fire. If he were a gentleman, he supposed he'd spare her this torturous raking of nearly extinguished coals. Something deeply internal and indefinable pushed him to forge ahead despite how unpleasant it was. Somehow, giving up looked bleaker than this.

"You don't salvage an agreement by walking away. You stay in the same room and hammer it out," he managed to say.

"What is there to salvage?" Adara charged with a pained throb in her voice. Her heart was lodged behind her collarbone like a sharp rock. Didn't he understand? Everything she'd brought to the table was gone.

Gideon only nodded at her chair, his expression shuttered yet insistent.

Adara dropped into her chair out of emotional exhaustion. For a few seconds she just sat there with her hands steepled before her face, eyes closed, drowning in despair.

"What do you *want,* Adara?"

She opened her eyes to find him statue hard across from her, expression unreceptive despite his demand she confide.

He was afraid it was something he couldn't give, she realized. Like love?

A barbed clamp snapped hard around her heart. She wasn't brave enough to give up that particular organ and had never fooled herself into dreaming a man could love her back, so no, she wouldn't ask him for love. She settled on part of the truth.

"I want to quit feeling so useless," she confessed, suffering the sensation of being stripped naked by the admission. "I'm predisposed to insecurity because of my upbringing, I know that. I'm not worthless, but I feel that way in this marriage. Now I can't even bring children into it. I can't live with this feeling of inadequacy, Gideon."

He stared hard at her for a long moment before letting out a snort of soul-crushing amusement.

Adara couldn't help her sharp exhale as she absorbed that strike. She tried to rise.

Gideon clamped his hand on her arm. "No. Listen. God, Adara…" He shook his head in bemusement, brow furrowed with frustration. "When you asked me to marry you—"

"Oh, don't!" she gasped, feeling her face flood with abashed color.

He tightened his grip on her wrist, keeping her at the table. "Why does that embarrass you? It's the truth. You came to me with the offer."

"I *know*. Which only reminds me how pathetically desperate I must have seemed. You didn't want me and wouldn't have chosen me if I hadn't more or less bribed you."

"Desperate?" he repeated with disbelief. "I was the desperate one, coming hat in hand to your father with a proposition I knew he'd laugh out of the room. All I had going for me was nerve."

"Someone else would have taken up the chance to invest with you, Gideon. It was a sound opportunity, which Papa saw after he got over being stubborn and shortsighted."

"After you worked on him."

She shook that off in a dismissive shrug, instantly self-conscious of the way she'd stood up for a man she'd barely known simply because she'd been intrigued by him. It had been quite a balancing act, truth be told.

"Don't pretend you didn't have anything to do with it." He sat forward. "Because this is what I'm trying to tell you. You came to me with things I didn't have. Your father's partnership. Entrée into the tightest and most influential Greek cartels in New York and Athens. I needed that, I wanted it, and I had no real belief I could actually get it."

"Well, I didn't have much else to offer, did I?" she pointed out in a remembered sense of inadequacy.

"Your virginity springs to mind, but we'll revisit that another time," he rasped, making her lock her gaze with his in shocked incredulity.

Suddenly, very involuntarily, she flashed back to her wedding night and the feel of his fingers touching her intimately, his mouth roaming from her lips to her neck to her breast and back as he teased her into wanting an even thicker penetration. She hadn't understood how his incredibly hard thrust could hurt and feel so good at the same time. Instead of being intimidated by his strength and weight, she'd basked in the sense of belonging as his solid presence moved above her, on her, and within her so smoothly, bringing such a fine tension into every cell of her being. His hard arms had surrounded and braced her, yet shielded her from all harm, making her feel safer than she'd ever felt in her life, so that when she'd shattered, she'd known he'd catch her.

Her body clenched in remembered ecstasy even as she was distantly aware of his hold on her gentling. He caressed her bare forearm and his voice lowered to the smoky tone he'd used when he'd told her how lovely she'd felt to him then. *So hot and sweet. So good.*

"Try to understand what it meant for me to form a connection to you."

Her scattered faculties couldn't tell if he was talking about her deflowering or the marriage in general. She shivered with latent arousal, pulling herself away from his touch to ground herself in the now.

"People knew I came from nothing," he said. "You want to know why I only speak Greek when I absolutely have to? Because my accent gives me away as the bottom class sailor that I am."

"It does not," she protested distractedly.

He reached to tuck a tendril of hair behind her ear, his touch lingering to trace lightly beneath her jaw. "If you want me to talk, you're going to have to listen. People respect you, Adara. Not because your father owned the company, not because of your wealth, but because of the way you conduct yourself. Everyone knew your father's faults and could see that you were above his habits of lashing out and making hasty decisions. They knew you were intelligent and fair and had influence with him."

"Now I know you're lying." She drew back, out of his reach.

"He didn't sway easily, that's true." He dropped his hands to his thighs. "But if anyone could change his mind, it was you. Everyone knew that, from the chambermaids to the suits in the boardroom. And people also knew that you were being very choosy about finding a husband. *Very* choosy."

He sat back, his demeanor solidifying into the man who headed so many boardroom tables, sharp and firm. Not someone you argued with.

"I didn't appreciate what that choosiness meant until I was by your side and suddenly I was being looked at like I had superpowers because you'd picked me. Maybe it sounds weak to say my ego needed that, but it did. I went from being an upstart no one trusted to a legitimate businessman. I had had some success before I met you, but once

I married you, *I* had self-worth because *you* gave it to me."

"But—" Her heart moved into her throat. She wanted to believe him, her inner being urgently needed to believe him, but it was so far from the way she perceived herself. "You're exaggerating."

"No, I'm telling you why I'm fighting to keep you."

"But people respect you. That won't go away if we divorce."

"*Now* they respect me. And perhaps that wouldn't go away overnight, although I can guarantee I'd be painted the villain if we split. People would pin the blame on me because you're nice and I'm not, but I'm not saying I want to stay married so I can continue using this knighthood you've unconsciously bestowed on me. It comes down to loyalty and gratitude and my own self-respect. I *like* being your husband. I want to keep the position."

"It's not a job." She'd tried to treat Husband and Wife like spots on an organizational chart and it wasn't that simple. Having a gorgeous body in a tux to escort her to fundraisers wasn't enough. She needed someone she could call when her world was crashing in on her and she thought she was dying.

That unexpected thought disturbed her. She had learned very young to guard her feelings, never show her loneliness, be self-sufficient and never, ever imagine her needs were important enough to be met. Wanting to rely on Gideon was a foreign concept, but it was there.

Gideon was watching her like a cat, ready to react, but what would he have done if he'd come home to find her sobbing her heart out? He'd have tried to ship her into the sterile care of stiff beds and objectifying instruments.

And yet, if she had found the courage to ask, would he have stayed with her and held her hand at the hospital? Would it have made a difference if he had?

It would have made a huge difference.

Deeply conflicted, she pushed back her chair, fingers knotting into the napkin on her lap. She didn't like feeling so tempted to try when there were so many other things wrong between them. "You make it sound so easy and it's not, Gideon."

"We have a few days before your brother shows up," he cut in with quick assertion. A muscle pulsed in his jaw. "I've cleared my schedule to the end of the week. We'll spend time together and set a new course. Turn this ship around."

She wanted to quirk a smile at the shipbuilder's oh-so-typical nautical reference, but her system was flooded with adrenaline, filling her with caution.

"What if—" She stopped herself, not wanting to admit she was terrified that spending time with him would increase her feelings for him. He was trying to make her feel special and it was working, softening her toward him. That scared her. If she knew anything about her husband, and she didn't know nearly enough, she knew he wasn't the least bit sentimental. She could develop feelings for him, but they'd never be returned.

What was his real reason for wanting to stay married?

"Look how much we've weathered and worked through since this morning," he reasoned with quiet persistence, showcasing exactly how he'd pushed a struggling shipyard into a dominant global enterprise in less than a decade. "We can make this marriage work for us, Adara. Give me a few days to prove it."

Days that were going to be excruciating even without a replay of today.

Nerves accosted her each time she thought of seeing Nico again and in the end, her consideration of Gideon's demand sprang from that. She would prefer to have him with her when she met Nico again. She couldn't explain it, but so many things, from social events to family dinners, were easier to face when Gideon was with her. She'd always felt that little bit more safe and confident when he was beside her, as if he had her back.

"You'd really move over to my brother's house with me?" she asked tentatively.

"Of course."

There was no "of course" about it. He showed up for the events in his calendar because it was their deal, not because he wanted to be there for her.

At least, that was her perception, but she hadn't really asked for anything more than that, had she? He'd offered to come to the hospital each time she'd told him about another miscarriage. She was the one who'd rebuffed the suggestion, hiding her feelings, not only holding him at a distance but pushing him away, too fearful of being vulnerable to even try to rely on him.

Which hadn't made her less vulnerable, just more bereft.

She couldn't stomach feeling that isolated again, not when she had so much of herself on the line. Still, she wasn't sure how to open herself up to help either.

"If you really want to, then okay. That's fine. But no guarantees," she cautioned. "I'm not making any promises."

He flinched slightly, but nodded in cool acceptance of her terms.

# CHAPTER FIVE

GIDEON WAS A bastard, in the old-fashioned sense of the word and quite openly in the contemporary sense. When he wanted something, he found a way to get it. He wasn't always fair about it. His "bastard" moniker was even, at times, prefaced with words like *ruthless, self-serving,* and *heartless.*

When it came to other men trying to exercise power over him, he absolutely was all of those things. He fought dirty when he had to and without compunction.

He had a functioning conscience, however, especially when it came to women and kids. When it came to his wife, he was completely sincere in wanting to protect her in every way.

Except if it meant shielding her from himself. When Adara's brother, "Nic," he had called himself, had invited them to take a room at his house, that was exactly what Gideon had heard. *A* room. *One* bed.

Normally he would never take up such an offer. Given the unsavory elements in his background, he kept to himself whenever possible. He liked his privacy and was also a man who liked his own personal space. Even at home in New York, he and Adara slept in separate beds in separate bedrooms. He visited hers; she never came to his. When she rose to shower after their lovemaking, he took his cue and left.

That had always grated, the way she disappeared before the sweat had dried on his skin, but it was the price of autonomy so he paid it.

*Had* paid it. He was becoming damn restless for entry into the space Adara occupied—willing to do whatever it took to invade it, even put himself into the inferior position of accepting a favor from a stranger.

Irritated by these unwanted adjustments to his rigidly organized life, he listened with half an ear to the vineyard manager's wife babble about housekeepers on vacation and stocked refrigerators, trying not to betray his impatience for her to get the hell out and leave them alone.

The nervous woman insisted on orienting them in the house, which looked from the outside like an Old English rabbit warren. Once inside, however, the floor plan opened up. Half the interior walls had been knocked out, some had been left as archways and pony walls, and the exterior ones along the back had been replaced by floor-to-ceiling windows. The remodeling, skilled as it was, was obvious to Gideon's sharp eye, but he approved. The revised floor plan let the stunning view of grounds, beach and sea become the wallpaper for the airy main-floor living space.

"The code for the guest wireless is on the desk in here," the woman prattled on as she led them up the stairs and pressed open a pair of double doors.

Gideon glanced into a modern office of sleek equipment, comfortable workspaces and a stylish, old-fashioned wet bar. A frosted crest was subtly carved into the mirrored wall behind it. In the back of his mind, he heard again the male voice identifying himself when he had called the hotel, the modulated voice vaguely familiar.

*It's Nic...Makricosta. I'm looking for my sister, Adara.* Gideon had put the tiny hesitation down to anything from nerves to distraction.

Now, as he recognized the crest, he put two and

two together and came up with C-4 explosive. A curse escaped him.

Both women turned startled gazes to where he lingered in the office doorway.

"You told me your brother had changed his name. I didn't realize to what," Gideon said, trying for dry and wry, but his throat had become a wasteland in the face of serious danger to his invented identity.

"Oh," Adara said with ingenuous humor. "I didn't realize I never..." A tiny smile of sheepish pride crept across her lips. "He's kind of a big deal, isn't he? It's one of the reasons I hesitated to get in touch. I thought he might dismiss me as a crackpot, or as someone trying to get money out of him."

*Kind of a big deal?* Nicodemus Marcussen was the owner and president of the world's largest media empire, not to mention a celebrated journalist in his own right. His work these days tended toward in-depth analysis of third-world coup d'état stuff, but he was no stranger to political exposés and other investigative reporting in print or on camera. Running a background check would be something he did between pouring his morning coffee and taking his first sip.

Gideon reassured himself Nic had no reason to do it, but tension still crawled though him as they continued their tour.

"My number is on the speed dial," the woman said to Adara. "Please call if you need anything. The Kyrios was most emphatic that you be looked after. He's hurrying his business in Athens as best he can, but it will be a couple of days before he's able to join you." She made the statement as she led them into a regal guest room brimming with fresh flowers, wine, a fruit basket, a private balcony with cushioned wicker furniture and a massive sleigh bed with a puffy white cover. "I trust you'll be comfortable?"

Gideon watched Adara count the number of beds in the room and become almost as pale as the pristine quilt. She looked to him, clearly expecting him to ask for a second room. Any day previous to this one he would have, without hesitation. Today he remained stubbornly silent.

Color crept under her skin as the silence stretched and she realized if anyone made an alteration to these arrangements, it would have to be her. He watched subtle, uncomfortable tension invade her posture and almost willed her to do it. He wanted to share her bed, but he suddenly saw exactly how hard it was for her to stand up for herself.

She gave a jerky little smile at the woman and said, "It's fine, thank you," and Gideon felt a pang of disappointment directed at himself. He should have made this easy for her. *But he didn't want to.*

The woman left. As the distant sound of the front door closing echoed through the quiet house, Adara looked to him as if he'd let her down.

"Do we just take another room?" A white line outlined her pursed mouth.

"Why would we need to?" he challenged lightly.

"We're not sharing a bed, Gideon." Hard and implacable, not like her at all.

"Why not?" he asked with a matching belligerence, exactly like himself because this issue was riling him right down to the cells at the very center of his being.

Her gaze became wild-eyed and full of angry anxiety. "Have you listened to me at all in the last twenty-four hours? *I don't want to get pregnant!*"

"People have felt that way for centuries. That's why they invented condoms," he retorted with equal ire. "I bought some before we left the hotel. Do you have an allergy to latex that I don't know about?"

She took a step back, her anger falling away so completely it took him aback. "I didn't think of that." Her brows came together in consternation. "You really wouldn't mind wearing one?"

He stood there flummoxed, utterly amazed. "You really didn't think of asking me to use them?"

"Well, you never have the whole time we've been married. I wasn't with anyone else before you. They're not exactly on my radar." She gave a defensive shrug of her shoulders, averting her gaze while a flush of embarrassment stained her cheekbones.

*Innocent,* he thought, and was reminded of another time when they'd stood in a bedroom, her nervous tension palpable while he was drowning in sexual hunger.

Anticipation was like a bed of nails in his back, pushing him toward her. On that first occasion, she had worn a blush-pink negligee and a cloak of reserve he'd enjoyed peeling away very, very slowly.

*Don't screw this up,* he'd told himself then, and reiterated it to himself today. The first night of their marriage, he'd had one chance to get their intimate relationship off on the right foot. He had one chance to press the reset button now.

The primal mate in him wanted to move across the room, kiss her into receptiveness and fall on the bed in a familiar act of simple, much-needed release.

But it wouldn't be enough. He saw it in the way her lashes flicked to his expression and she read the direction of his thoughts. Rather than coloring in the pretty way he so enjoyed watching when he suggested a visit to her room, she paled a little and her lips trembled before she bit them together.

"You don't…" Licking her lips, she looked to him with huge eyes that nearly brimmed with defensiveness. "You don't expect me to fall into bed with you just because you've got a condom, do you?"

Expect it? The animal in him howled, *Yes.*

"It's always been good, hasn't it?" He bit out the words, perhaps a little too confrontational, but his confidence was unexpectedly deserting him.

She crossed her arms, shoulders so tight he

thought she'd snap herself in half. "It's always been fine."

"Fine?" he charged, gutted by the faint praise.

She sent him a helpless look that made him feel like a bully.

"I can hardly deny that I've enjoyed it, can I?" she said, but the undertone of something like embarrassment or shame stole all the excitement he might have felt if she'd said it another way. "I just…"

"Don't trust me." He ground out the words with realization. It was an unexpectedly harsh blow. "Come on," he said, holding out his hand before he lost what was left of his fraying self-control.

She stilled with guardedness. "What? Where?"

"Anywhere but this room or I'll be all over you and you're obviously not ready for that."

A funny little frisson went through Adara as she took in the rugged, intimidating presence that was her husband. He held out a commanding hand, as imperious and inscrutable as ever, but his words had an undercurrent of…was it compassion?

Whatever it was, it did things to her, softening her, but it scared her at the same time. She was already too susceptible to him.

And his desire for her was a seduction in itself. Her insecurity as a woman had been ramped to maximum with everything that had happened, but things had shifted in the last twenty-four hours. She was looking at him, hearing him. His sexual hunger wasn't an act. She knew the signs of interest and excitement in him. His chiseled features were tense with focus. A light flush stained his cheekbones—almost a flag of temper if not for the line of his mouth softened into a hungry, feral near smile.

Her body responded the way it always did, skin prickling with a yearning to be stroked, breasts tightening, loins clenching in longing for him.

Oh, God. If she stayed in this room, she'd *beg* him to be all over her, and where would that lead beyond a great orgasm? She didn't know what sort of relationship she wanted with Gideon, but knew unequivocally she couldn't go back to great sex and nothing else.

She moved to the door, not expecting him to fall in beside her and take her hand. A *zing* of excitement went through her as he enveloped her narrow fingers in his strong grasp. Stark defenselessness flared and she wanted to pull herself away. Why?

"It's not that I distrust you," she said, trying to convince herself as much as him while they walked down the stairs, her hand like a disembodied limb she was so aware of it in his. "I know you'd never hurt me. You can be stubborn and bossy, but you're not cruel." It still felt strange to speak her mind so openly, increasing her sense of vulnerability and risk. Her heart tremored.

"But you don't trust me with who you *are*," he goaded lightly.

Her hand betrayed her, wriggling self-consciously in his firm grip. He eyed her knowingly as he reached with his free hand to slide open the glass door on the back of the house.

An outdoor kitchen was tucked to the side of a lounge area. A free-form pool glittered a few steps away, half in the sun, the rest in the shadow of the house. The paving stones dwindled past it to a meandering path down the lawn to the beach. The grounds were bordered on one side by the vineyard and by an orange grove on the other.

"Swim?" he suggested as they stood at the edge of the pool staring into the hypnotic stillness of the turquoise water.

Working up her courage, she asked softly, "Do you trust *me,* Gideon?"

His hold on her loosened slightly and his mouth twitched with dismay. "I don't wholly trust anyone," he admitted gruffly. "It's not because I don't think you're trustworthy. It's me. The way I'm made."

"The "it's not you, it's me" brush-off. There's a firm foundation." Disgruntled, she would have walked away, but he tightened his hold on her hand and followed her into the sunshine toward the orange grove.

"Would it help to know that I've been more open with you than I've been with anyone else in my life? Ever? Perhaps you learned to keep your feelings to yourself because you were afraid of how your father would react, but after my mother died, no one responded to what I wanted or needed. Even when she was alive, she was hardly there. Not her fault, but I've had to be completely self-sufficient most of my life. It shocks me every time you appear to genuinely care what I'm thinking or feeling."

The sheer lonesomeness of what he was saying gouged a furrow into her heart. She might have a stilted relationship with her younger brothers, but they would be there if she absolutely needed them. She unconsciously tightened her hand on his and saw a subtle shift in his stony expression, as if her instinctive need to comfort him had the opposite effect, making him uncomfortable.

"You never talk about your mom. She was a single mother? Constantly working to make ends meet?"

His face became marble hard. "A child. I have a memory of asking her how old she was and she said twenty-one. That doesn't penetrate when you're young. It sounds ancient, but if I can remember it, I was probably five or six, which puts her pregnant at fifteen or sixteen. I suspect she was a runaway, but I've never tried to investigate. I don't think I'd like any of the answers."

She understood. At best, his mother might have been shunned by her family for a teen pregnancy, forcing her to leave her home; at worst, he could be the product of rape.

A little chill went through her before she asked, "What happened after you lost her? Where did you go?"

His mouth pressed tight.

Her heart fell. This was one of those times he wouldn't answer.

He surprised her by saying gruffly, "There was a sailor who was decent to me."

"A kindly old salt?" she asked, starting to smile.

"The furthest thing from it. My palms would be wet with broken blisters and all he'd say was, 'There's no room for crybabies on a ship,' and send me back to work."

She gasped in horror, checking her footstep to pause and look at him.

He shook his head at her concern. "It's true. It wasn't a cruise liner. If you're not crew, you're cargo and cargo has to pay. If he hadn't pushed me, I wouldn't be where I am today. He taught me the ropes—that's not a pun. Everything from casting off to switching out the bilge pump. He taught me how to hang on to my money, not drink or gamble it away. Even how to fight. Solid life skills."

"Does he know where you are today? What you've made of yourself?"

"No." His stoic expression flinched and his tone went flat. "He died. He was mugged on a dock for twenty American dollars. Stabbed and left to bleed to death. I came back too late to help him."

"Oh, Gideon." She wanted to bring his hand to her aching heart. Of course he was reticent and hard-edged with that sort of pain in his background. Questions bubbled in her mind. How old had he been? What had he done next?

She bit back pressing him. Baby steps, she reminded herself, but baby steps toward what? Their marriage was broken because *they* were broken.

She frowned. The future they'd mapped out with such simplistic determination five years ago had mostly gone according to plan. When it came to goal achievement in a materialistic sense, they were an unstoppable force. A really great team.

But what use was a mansion if no patter of tiny feet filled it? Without her father goading for expansion, she was content to slow the pace and concentrate on fine-tuning what they had.

She wasn't sure what she wanted from her marriage, only knew she couldn't be what Gideon seemed to expect her to be.

Where could they go from here?

The sweet scent of orange blossoms coated the air as they wandered in silence between the rows of trees. Gideon lazily reached up to steal a flower from a branch and brought it to his nose. A bemused smile tugged at his lips.

"Your hair smelled like this on our wedding night."

Adara's abdomen contracted in a purely sensual kick of anticipation, stunning her with the wash of acute hunger his single statement provoked. She swallowed, trying to hide how such a little thing as him recalling that could affect her so deeply.

"I wore a crown of them," she said, trying to sound light and unaffected.

"I remember." He looked at her in a way that swelled the words with meaning, even though she wasn't sure what the meaning was.

A flood of pleasure and self-consciousness brimmed up in her.

"That almost sounds sentimental, but the night can only be memorable for how awkward I was," she dismissed, accosted anew by embarrassment at how gauche and inexperienced she'd been.

"Nervous," he corrected. "As nervous as you are now." He halted her and stood in front of her to drift the petal of the flower down her cheek, leaving a tickling, perfumed path. "So was I."

"I'm sure," she scoffed, lips coming alive under the feathery stroke of the blossom. She licked the sensation away. "What are you doing?"

"Seducing you. It'd be nice if you noticed."

She might have smiled, but he distracted her by brushing the flower under her chin. She lifted to escape the disturbing tickle and he stole a kiss.

It was a tender press of his mouth over hers, not demanding and possessive as she'd come to expect from him. This was more like those first kisses they'd shared a lifetime ago, during their short engagement. Brief and exploratory. Patient.

Sweet but frustrating. She was too schooled in how delicious it was to give in to passion to go back to chaste premarital nuzzling.

He drew back and looked into her eyes through a hooded gaze. "I remember every single thing about that night. How soft your skin was." The blossom dropped away as he stroked the back of his bent fingers down her cheek and into the crook of her neck. His gaze went lower and his hand followed. "I remember how I had to learn to be careful with your nipples because they're so sensitive."

They were. Sensitive and responsive. Tightening now so they poked against the dual layers of bra and shirt, standing out visibly and seeming to throb as he lightly traced a finger around the point of one. A whimper of hungry distress escaped her.

"I remember that most especially." The timbre of his voice became very low and intense. "The little noises of pleasure you made that got me so hot because it meant you liked what I was doing to you. I almost lost it the first time you came. Then you fell apart again when I was inside you and you were so tight—"

"Gideon, stop!" She grasped the hand that had drifted to the button at the waistband of her shorts. Her lungs felt as if all the air in them had evaporated and a distinctive throb pulsed between her thighs.

"I don't want to stop," he growled with masculine ferocity. "The only thing hotter than our first time together has been every time since."

She wanted to believe that, but yesterday...

Gideon watched Adara withdraw and knew he was losing her. He'd come on too strong, but hunger for her was like a wolf in him, snapping and predatory from starvation.

"What's wrong?" he demanded, then swore silently at himself when he saw that his roughened tone made her flinch. He wasn't enjoying these heart-to-hearts any more than she was, but they were necessary. He accepted that, but it was hard. He was the type to attack, not expose his throat.

Adara flicked him a wary glance and stepped back, arms crossing her chest in the way he was beginning to hate because it shut him out so effectively. She chewed her bottom lip for a few seconds before cutting him another careful glance.

"Yesterday you said… Maybe I'm being oversensitive, but what you said when we were swimming really hurt, Gideon. About me not being good enough. I *try* to give you as much pleasure as you give me—"

He cut her off with a string of Greek epithets that should have curled the leaves off the surrounding trees. "Yesterday was a completely different era in this relationship. What I said—" The chill of frustration gripped his vital organs. How could he explain that his appetite for her went beyond what even seemed human? He understood now why she'd confined their relations to oral sex, but it didn't change the fact that he ached constantly for release inside her. "I felt managed, Adara. I don't say that with blame. I'm only telling you how it seemed from what I knew then. I want you. Not other women. Not tarts like Lexi. *You.* Having you hold yourself back from me made me nuts. I need you to be as caught up as I am. To want me. It's the only way I can cope with how intense my need for you is."

She blinked at him in shock.

He rubbed a hand down his face, wishing he could wipe away his blurted confession. "If that scares the hell out of you, then I'm sorry. I probably shouldn't have told you."

"No," she breathed, head shaking in befuddlement. "But I find it hard to believe you feel like that. I'm not a siren. You're the one with all the experience, the one who thinks about using condoms because you've used them before."

"Yes, I have," he said with forcible bluntness, not liking how defensive he felt for having a sexual history when she'd come to him pristine and pure. "But you know when the last time I used one was? The night before we met. I don't remember much about the woman I was dating then, only that the next evening she left me because I asked her if she knew anything about you. Pretty crass, I know. I couldn't stop thinking about you."

Her searching gaze made him extremely uncomfortable. He jerked his chin.

"Let's keep walking."

"And talking? Because it's such fun?" Adara bent
to retrieve the blossom he'd dropped and twirled
it beneath her nose as they continued deeper into
the orange grove. His revelations were disturbing
on so many levels, most especially because they
were creating emotional intimacy, something that
was completely foreign to their marriage. Nevertheless, as painful as it was to dredge up her hurts,
she was learning that it was cathartic to acknowledge them. Letting him explain his side lessened
the hurt.

She glanced at him as they walked, no longer
touching.

"I hate thinking of you with other women." The
confession felt like a barbed hook dragged all the
way from the center of her heart across the back
of her throat. "Infidelity destroyed our family. We
were quite normal at first, then Nico was sent
away and it was awful. Both my parents drank.
My father fooled around and made sure my mother
knew about it. She was devastated. So much yell-

ing and crying and fighting. I never wanted any-thing like that to happen to me."

"It won't," he assured her, reaching across with light fingers to smooth her hair off her shoulder so he could tuck his hand under the fall of loose tresses and cup the back of her neck. "But tell me you were jealous of Lexi anyway. My ego needs it."

"I felt insecure and useless," she said flatly.

He checked his step and a spasm of pain flashed across his face before he seared her with a look. "Exactly how I felt when I saw you walk up the driveway here. Like I'd been rejected because I wasn't good enough."

She bit her lips together in compunction while her heart quivered in her chest, shimmering with the kind of pain a seed must feel before the first shoot breaks through its shell. She wanted to cry and throw herself into him and run away and pro-tect herself.

"We're never going to be able to make this work, Gideon. I don't want the power to hurt you any more than I want you to be able to hurt me. This is a mess. We're messing each other up and it's going to be—"

"Messy?" he prompted dryly. "Just take it one day at a time, Adara. That's all we can do."

She drew in and released a shaken breath, nodding tightly as they kept walking. Their steps made soft crunches in the dry grass while cicadas chirped in accompaniment. No breeze stirred beneath the trees and the heat clutched the air in a tight grip.

"Should we go back and swim?" she suggested.

"If you like."

It didn't matter what they did, she realized. They were filling time until her brother returned, distracting themselves while sexual attraction struggled for supremacy over hurt and misgivings. They should give in. Sex would take the edge off their tension and God knew she wanted him. Lovemaking with Gideon was a transcendent experience as far as she was concerned.

But she'd never felt this vulnerable with him before. It made physical intimacy seem that much more *intimate*. Her normal defenses were a trampled mess. The idea of letting him touch her and watch her lose control was terrifying. He'd see how much he meant to her and that was too much to bear.

Twenty minutes later they were in the pool. His laps were a purposeful crawl with flip turns and patterned breathing, hers a less disciplined breast-stroke that made one lap to his four. Tiring, she moved to sit on one of the long tile stairs in the shallow end, half out of the water as she watched him. The pool was fully shaded now, leaving her quite comfortable watching his athletic build cut through the water.

When he stopped and joined her on the step, he was breathing heavily, probably having swum a mile though she'd lost count ages ago, distracted by the steady thrust of his arms into the water and the tight curve of his buttocks as he kicked. She really couldn't fathom what a sexy, virile man like him was doing with mousy, boring her.

And even though he'd pushed himself with thirty minutes of hard swimming, his gaze moved restlessly, as if he was looking for the next challenge.

"You're not comfortable with downtime, are you?" she said.

He glanced questioningly at her while diamond droplets glittered on his face and chest hair.

"You're driven," she expounded. "I keep thinking of all those plans we made, but what does it matter if we have a floating hotel? I know it's top-notch, but who cares? We don't need the money and the world doesn't need another behemoth cruise ship."

"It matters to the people we've employed and the ones who invested with us. But you're right, I suppose. Wealth isn't something either of us really needs. Not anymore. It's a habit I've fallen into, I guess."

"You worked hard to get here and now you don't know how to stop," she paraphrased.

He made a noise of agreement.

"If we don't have children, what would we fill our lives with? More hotels and boats?" Involuntarily, her ears strained to hear the words *each other*.

They didn't come. After a long moment he said, "Our last five-year plan took months to mold. This one can, too. There's no rush."

"There is," she insisted. "I feel like if we don't have everything sorted out before we sleep together again, our marriage will go back to the way it was and I'll be stuck in it." There. She'd said it. Her worst fear had blurted out of her.

He stared at her for a long minute, absorbing her

outburst, then he chuckled softly and shook his head. "And I can't think of anything but making love to you again. New plans?" He shook his head as if she was speaking another language. "We're at quite an impasse."

He wasn't being dismissive, just blatantly honest. Her heart constricted as she absorbed that this was what he'd meant about trusting him. Somehow she had to dredge up the faith to believe he'd continue working on their marriage along with the courage to surrender herself to him. The potential for pain was enormous.

While the yearning to feel close to him was unbearable.

She looked up to where the afternoon sun had bleached the clear sky to nearly white. Not even close to evening or bedtime. She hadn't brought either her green-light or red-light nightgown. How else could she possibly signal to him that she was receptive to his advances?

*Oh, Adara, quit being such a priss.* They were learning to *communicate,* weren't they?

Her internal lecture didn't stop her heart from beating frantically in her throat as she set tentative fingertips on his wrist where it rested on his thigh. Leaning toward him, she shielded her eyes with a swoop of her lashes and watched his lips part slightly in surprise before she pressed hers to them.

Heat flooded into her. The very best kind of heat that had nothing to do with Greek sunshine and everything to do with this man's chemistry interacting with hers. He didn't move, letting her control the pressure and deepening of their kiss, but he responded with a muted groan of approval and drew on her tongue with gentle suction.

Runnels of sexual hunger poured through her system, spreading out in delicate fingers that excited her senses and made her want to tip into his lap.

Shakily she pulled back and licked the taste of him off her lips before she gripped the railing in slippery fingers and forced her weak knees to take her weight as she stood.

"Will you, um, give me a minute to shower before you come up?" The question was so uncouched and blatant she felt as though she'd stripped herself naked here in public.

"I'll use the shower in the cabana and be up in

ten," he replied gruffly, eyes like lasers that peeled her bathing suit from her body.

Adara wrapped a towel around herself and went to their room.

# CHAPTER SIX

THE PARALLEL TO their first time kept ringing in Gideon's skull. He was just as keyed up as he'd been then, his masculine need to possess twitching in him like an electric wire, while his ego inched out onto that wire, precarious as a tightrope walker.

*No room for false moves.* The message pulsed as a current, back and forth within him.

He climbed the stairs as though pulled by an invisible force. No matter how many times he told himself it was ridiculous to place so much importance on this—he'd done this before. *They* had. It didn't matter. This meant something. The last time he'd felt this sense of magnitude, Adara's initiation to sexual maturity had been on the line. He'd felt a massive responsibility to make it good for her, especially as he'd been selfishly determined he would be her only lover for the rest of their lives.

The pressure to ensure they were both satisfied with that exclusivity had been enormous.

Without being too egotistical, he believed they had been. He certainly had. Her subtle beauty had flourished into his own private land of enchantment.

This ought to be a visit to the familiar, he told himself as he turned the handle on the door and pressed into their room. It wasn't. This was uncharted territory and the initiation this time was happening to both of them, moving them into some kind of emotional maturity he would have rather avoided. The tightrope he was walking didn't even feel as if it was there anymore. He was walking across thin air, reminding himself not to look down or he'd be tumbling into a bottomless crevasse.

As he leaned on the door until it clicked, she opened the bathroom door and emerged wearing one of his T-shirts. The soft white cotton clung to her damp curves and naked breasts before falling to the tops of her thighs. He couldn't tell if she wore underpants and couldn't wait to find out.

"I didn't bring anything sexy," she murmured apologetically, her eyes bigger than the black plums in the basket. Her apprehension was unmistakable.

"You look edible," he said, voice originating somewhere deep in his chest. He moved across to her. "I didn't shave." He took her hand and rubbed the heel across his jaw where a hint of stubble was coming in.

"It's okay," she murmured and pulled her hand back then wrung it with her other one. "I'm sorry. I don't know why I'm so terrified. This is silly."

A swell of tenderness rose in him. He took her hands and kissed each palm. "It's okay. I'll take it slow. As slow as the first time. I want to savor every second."

Her smile trembled. "I know it will be good, but my body seems to think we're strangers. I keep reminding myself I know everything about you. The important things, anyway."

His blood stopped in his arteries as he thought about what she didn't know about him. Important things, but so was this. He needed to cement their connection before he could even contemplate stressing it with a full exposure of who he was. And wasn't.

Adara cupped the sides of his head, trembling

with nerves and anticipation, wanting the kiss that would erase all her angst and drown her in the sea of erotic sensations he always delivered.

Gideon wasn't moving, seeming to have slipped behind a veil of some kind.

"What's wrong?" she asked as doubts began to intrude.

"Nothing," he said gruffly and set his mouth on hers.

The first contact was just that, contact. Like finding the edge of the pool when your eyes were closed and head submerged and your lungs ready to give up. Relief poured through her as the familiar shape and give of his full lips compressed her own.

And then he opened his mouth in a familiar signal that she do the same and she nearly melted into a puddle of homecoming joy. His arms slid around her and pulled her into a hard embrace against his shirtless chest, muscles bulging with such strength it was almost uncomfortably hard against her tender breasts, but so welcome.

Adara curled her arms around the back of his neck and clung, kissing him unreservedly as her senses absorbed every delicious thing about him.

His shoulders and back were gloriously smooth and naked, scented with body wash and rippling hotly as he moved his hands on her, awakening every nerve in her body.

The wide plant of his strong legs let her feel the brush of his hairy legs against the smoothness of her thighs. She wriggled closer, wanting to feel the hard muscle that told her he liked the feel of her against him. Her body craved contact with that gorgeous erection and she arched herself into firm pressure against the ridge she could feel behind the fly of his shorts.

"This isn't slow," he growled, straightening and grasping a handful of T-shirt between her shoulder blades.

The soft fabric stretched across the round thrust of her breasts. Her nipples stood out prominently. Eagerly. He leaned to take one in his mouth, suckling her through the fabric until she let out a keening moan of distress at the pleasure-pain. He pulled back to examine the wet stain that turned the cotton invisible, clearly revealing the sharp pink tip and shaded areola of her breast.

Adara gasped at how flagrantly erotic this was, but couldn't help arching a little in pride when she could see how excited he was by the sight. He smiled tightly before bending to do the same to her other nipple, bringing her up on her toes the sensation was so ferociously strong. A ripple of near ecstasy quavered in her abdomen, making her weak and mindless. She clung to him as if he was a life raft.

"I've always liked that, too," he said with satisfaction.

"What?" she asked breathily.

"The way you dig your kitten claws into me when you're about to come."

The heat that suffused her nearly burned her alive. "I'm not," she said in a near strangle.

"No?" A light of determination flared behind the liquid heat that had turned his dark eyes black.

Her heart skipped in alarm, but his superior strength easily backed her to the bed and levered her into the poofy cloud of the duvet. He took a moment to admire the purple undies she was wearing, the prettiest pair she'd brought, before he drew them down her legs in a deliberately slow tease of satin against skin.

The unfettered daylight and proprietary touch

of his strong hands on her legs made her thighs quiver.

"Gideon," she protested.

"You're so close, *matia mou*," he cajoled, thumb stroking into her wet folds to search out the knot of sensation that was undeniably eager for his touch. She instinctively lifted her hips off the bed at the first contact. He bent and chuckled softly against her inner thigh, kissing his way to where her entire world was centered.

Latent modesty curled her fingers into his hair and she moaned indecisively, wanting badly to give in to what he offered, but she felt like such a wanton. She tossed her head back and forth, tugged on his hair, then felt the hot lick of his tongue and nearly screamed with delight. Need ravaged through her and she encouraged him, nearly begged him with the rock of her hips and clench of her fist in his hair and then—

Release seared through her like a white-hot blade, blinding in its intensity. Sensations racked her on waves of unadulterated pleasure that gripped her for an eternity, exquisite and joyous.

She came back on a sobbing pant of gratification. Aftershocks trembled through her as she became aware of Gideon kissing his way up her torso, pushing aside the T-shirt. He lifted onto an elbow to admire the quivering breasts he'd bared, then slowly lifted his gaze to her face.

Adara felt utterly defenseless and he made it worse when he said, "Now imagine how you would feel if I left you right now."

The way she had been leaving him in exactly this state for weeks.

He began to roll away and her world crashed in. "Don't!" she cried.

He showed her the condom he'd reached for. "I can't," he said with a near-bitter fatalism. He opened his shorts and pushed them down, kicking his shorts free.

The thrust of his erection was as powerfully intimidating as ever, but she positively melted with anticipation. "Can I—" She tried to help him with the condom.

"Next time, Adara. For God's sake, just let me get inside you."

He lifted to cover her, his weight a sweet dominance as he pushed into her, filling her with the heat of his length and rocking his hips so he was seated as deeply as possible. Then he weaved his fingers into her hair and nuzzled light kisses on her brow and cheekbones, giving her time to adjust to his penetration.

"You don't know what it's been like," he grumbled.

She had an idea. Her body was barely hers, responding to the feel of him so strongly that just the thick stretch of him inside her and the faint friction of their tiniest movement was setting off another detonation. It would have been humiliating if it wasn't so amazingly, sweetly incredible.

"Oh, God, Gideon. I'm sorry," she moaned and scratched at his rib cage as she tilted her hips for more pressure and shuddered into ecstasy beneath his weight.

"Oh, babe," he said consolingly against her lips, rocking lightly to increase the sensations, forcing and prolonging her climax. "You missed this, too."

She shattered, unable to stop herself gasping in joy

"Don't be arrogant," she warned a minute later, turning her face to the side in discomfiture as she tried to catch her breath.

"I'm not, I swear I'm not." His breath was hot

on her ear before his tongue painted wet patterns on her nape.

"You don't seem quite as swept away as I am," she said pointedly, pressing against the wall of his chest.

"I'm barely hanging on. Can't you feel me shaking? If I was naked, I'd have been lost on the first thrust. Being inside you is so good, babe. I never want to leave. It's always like this, like I'm in heaven."

Her heart seemed to flower open to him and her hands moved on him of their own volition, absorbing that he was, indeed, trembling with strain.

"I thought I was the one shivering," she confessed softly.

"I live for this, Adara. The feel of you under me, the way you smell, the heat and the insane pleasure of feeling you around me." He pressed deep as he spoke, sparking a flare of need in her for another and another of those fiercely possessive thrusts.

"Don't stop," she begged. "It feels too good."

With an avid groan, he took her mouth in a deep soul kiss and thrust in a purposeful, primal rhythm. The sensations were nearly too much for her, but she couldn't let him go, couldn't give it up.

Her legs locked around him and her heels urged him to heavier, harder slams of his hips into hers. This wasn't a man initiating a virgin; it was too halves trying to meld into a whole. The sensations were acute and glorious and feral.

And when the culmination arrived, it was a simultaneous crescendo that burst from the energy between them, surrounding and sealing them in a halo of shimmering joy as they clung tightly to the only thing left in the universe. Each other.

Gideon left Adara at a complete and utter loss. She always left the bed first, hitting the shower so she could recover her defenses after letting them fall away during sex. Lovemaking always made her feel vulnerable, and after acting so greedily and helpless to her desire for him, she needed alone time more than ever. She'd never felt so peeled down to the core in her life

But Gideon disappeared into the bathroom, stealing her favorite line of escape. She sat up, thinking to dress, but then go where?

The toilet flushed and she flicked the corner of the duvet over her nudity, not sure where to look when he came out of the bathroom. He struck a pose in the doorway with elbows braced and a near belligerence in his naked stance.

"What's wrong?" she asked, unnerved by his intense stare.

"Nothing. You?" He seemed almost confrontational and it got her back up.

"No. Of course not." Except that she'd pretty much exploded in his arms and didn't know how to handle facing down this tough guy who didn't seem to have a shred of tenderness in him anymore. She slid a foot to the edge of the bed. "I'll, um, just have a quick shower—"

"Why?" he challenged. "You just had one."

True, but where else did one ever have complete privacy except the bathroom? She'd figured that one out in grade school. It was one of her coping strategies to this day. She set her chin, trying to think up a suitable way to insist.

"I hate it when you run away after sex," he said, coming toward the bed in a stealthy, pantherlike stride. "Unless you're inviting me to join you in the shower, stay exactly where you are."

Her heart skipped, reacting to both his looming presence and the shock of his words.

"You're the one who started it, running out

like you had a train to catch the first night of our honeymoon. I thought that's how we did this," she defended, going hot with indignation. "When we're done, we're done."

"Our first night was your first *time*. If I hadn't left you, I'd have made love to you all night and I didn't want to hurt you any more than I already had." He leaned over her as he spoke, forcing her onto her back.

She pressed a hand to his chest, warding him off. "Well, I didn't know that, did I? You walked out on me and I didn't like it, so I made it a habit to be the first to leave every other time."

He hung over her on straight arms, his eyes narrowed hawkishly. "So you're not running away to wash the feel of me off your skin?"

"No." That was absurd. She loved the feel and smell of him lingering on her. "Sometimes I run the shower but don't get in," she admitted sheepishly.

He muttered a curse of soft, frustrated amusement. "Then why…?"

"You make me feel like I can't resist you! Like all you have to do is look at me or say a word and

I'll melt onto my back. That's not a comfortable feeling."

"That's exactly how I want you to be. I want you here, under me. I want to make love to you until we're so weak we can't lift our heads. I've never been comfortable with how insatiable I am for you. At least if we're in the same boat, I can stand it."

She almost told him then that sometimes she woke in the middle of the night and ached for him to come to her. Shyness stopped her, but she overcame it enough to reach up to the back of his head and urge him down to kiss her. She stayed on her back, under him, and moaned in welcome as he settled his hot weight on her.

He groaned in gratification.

Moonlight allowed Adara to find his T-shirt on the floor. The doors were still open and the air had cooled off to a velvety warmth that caressed her nudity. She took a moment to savor the feel of her sensitive skin stroked by the night air. It was an uncharacteristic moment of sensuality for her.

She glanced at her naked form in the mirror. The woman staring back at her through the shadows was a bit of a stranger. The dark marks of Gideon's fingerprints spotted her buttocks and thighs. They'd got a little wild at times through the afternoon and evening, definitely more voracious than either had ever revealed to the other before.

Her abdomen fluttered in speculative delight. His focus on her had shored up places inside her that had been unsteady and ready to collapse. Her footing felt stronger now, even if the rest of her still swayed and trembled.

Yes, there were still places inside her that were sensitive and vulnerable, places very close to her heart. In some ways, she was even more terrified than she'd been before they'd come up here and thrown themselves at each other, but she was glad they'd made love. Very glad.

A whisper of movement drew her glance to the bed. Gideon's arm swept her space on the bed. The covers had long been thrown off and the bottom sheet was loose from the corners. They had indisputably wrecked this bed.

The body facedown upon it, however, was exquisitely crafted to withstand the demands he'd made upon it. Adara took a mental photo of his form in the bluish light: his muscled shoulders, the slope of his spine, the taut globes of his buttocks, his lean legs, one crooking toward her vacant spot as he came up on an elbow.

His expression relaxed as he spotted her in the middle of the room. She tightened her grasp on the T-shirt she clutched to her front.

"Get back here."

The smoky timbre of his voice was a rough caress all its own, while his imperious demand made her want to grin. Despite being a naturally dominant male, he usually phrased his commands as requests when he spoke to her. That was all part of the distance between them, she realized. Part of both of them not letting the other see the real person. She ought to be affronted by his true, domineering and dictatorial colors, but she liked that he wasn't quelling that piece of his personality around her anymore.

She liked even more that she wasn't afraid of this side of him. He wasn't an easy man to resist on any level, but she wasn't afraid to stand up to him.

Even if he still made her feel inordinately shy.

"I'm thirsty. And I want to see what's in these baskets." She turned away, prickles of awareness telling her he studied her back and bottom exactly as proprietarily as she'd looked at him before he'd woken. She shrugged his T-shirt over herself.

"That's the first thing I noticed about you and I hardly ever get to see it naked."

"My bum?" Her buttocks tightened beneath the light graze of his T-shirt and she felt herself heat. She turned to bring the basket along with the wineglasses to the bed, not bothering with the wine itself. She was after the sparkling water in the green bottle.

As she placed the basket on the bed and knelt across from him, she caught a look of disgruntlement on his face.

"All of you," he clarified. "You're gorgeous and I like looking at you."

She didn't know what to say. She was flattered, but only half believed him.

Tucking her loose hair behind her ear, she confided, "I've never felt confident about the way I look. Showing any hint of trying to be sexy while my father was alive would have been a one-way ticket to hell. And I never really trusted any man enough to flirt." She gave him the bottle of water to open for her then poured two glasses, drinking greedily only to make herself hiccup.

She giggled and covered her wet lips, but sobered as she saw Gideon glowering into his glass.

"Men who hit women make me insane. I know it's not right to answer violence with violence, but if your father were still alive, the police would be involved right now, one way or another." He took a deep slug of his water, eyes remaining hooded, not meeting her shocked gaze.

His vehemence was disturbing, prompting an odd need to comfort him. She reached across to stroke his tense arm. "Gideon, it's in the past. It's okay."

"No, it's not," he said sharply, but when he looked at her, his expression softened a little. "But right now isn't the time to think about it. Get rid of that," he ordered with a jerk of his chin at the T-shirt.

"What am I? Your sex slave now?" She did feel a little enslaved, but she wasn't as resentful as she ought to be about it.

"No. You're my wife. You ought to be comfortable letting me see you naked." He set aside his glass to reach for an orange.

She finished her own water and set it aside before easing the shirt off her body and setting it aside while she continued to kneel demurely, feet alongside her buttock, arm twitching to cover her breasts. To distract herself, she watched Gideon efficiently section the orange and bring a piece to his mouth.

He clutched it in his teeth and looked at her. "Bite," he said around it.

Her heart did a somersault. "Why?" The defensive question came automatically, but then she thought, *Just do it,* and leaned down to close her mouth on the fruit.

They bit it in half at the same time. Tangy juice exploded in her mouth. At the same time, his firm lips moved on hers in an erotic, openmouthed kiss. When she would have pulled away in surprise, he set a hand behind her head and kept her close enough to enjoy the messy, sweet, thorough act of sinful wickedness.

When he finally let her pull away to finish chewing and swallow, he grinned. "You flirt just fine, Mrs. Vozaras."

"Do it again," she blurted, making herself be assertive so she'd quit letting habits of inhibition hold her back from what she wanted.

A flicker of surprise flashed in his eyes before

his eyelids grew heavy and his gaze sexily watchful. In her periphery, she was aware of him growing hard and her mouth watered for that too, but she took another bite of orange and splayed her hand on his chest, leaning into him to enjoy the sticky, tart kiss.

The last shreds of her inhibitions fell away and they didn't get back to the orange for a long, long time.

"You're going to burn," Gideon said as he returned from the waves to see the sun had moved and the backs of Adara's legs were exposed to the intense rays.

She stayed on her stomach on the blanket, unmoved and unmoving, only blinking her eyes open sleepily, as if she didn't have an ounce of energy in her. Forty-eight hours of unfettered lovemaking, impulsive napping and abject laziness were taking a toll on both of them. His own ambition had frittered into an *I'll look at it later* attitude. He'd left his phone and tablet up at the house, bringing only his sunglasses and wife to the beach.

"I like being on vacation," she told him, still not moving.

He adjusted the umbrella so she was fully in the shade then flopped down beside her. "So do I. We should definitely do this more often."

A shadow passed behind her eyes before she lowered her lashes to hide it. She shifted to rest her chin on her stacked fists, the circumspect silence making him aware of all the things they'd avoided while enriching their knowledge of each other's capacity for physical pleasure. Suddenly they were back in the pool, he couldn't think beyond his sexual hunger, and she was telling him that she needed to know where their relationship was going.

Restless frustration moved through him. He didn't know what to tell her. This was perfect. Wasn't it? He couldn't think of one thing they needed besides warm sand, the reassuring swish of a calm sea, each other's heated breath while they—

A faint noise lifted his head and a preternatural tingle went through him as he noticed a speck appear in the distant sky. They hadn't been tracking time, neither of them particularly interested in a return to reality, but apparently it was descending whether they were ready for it or not.

"Babe? I think your brother's here."

# CHAPTER SEVEN

GIVEN HOW THEIR trip to Greece had started, Gideon supposed he shouldn't be surprised by Adara's reaction, but the way she paled and panicked startled him. She took herself back to the house as if her skin was on fire. In their room, she pulled on a sundress and revealed a level of agitation he'd never seen as the thwack of chopper blades became loud enough to make the house hum.

He dragged on shorts and a collared shirt, concerned by the way her hand shook as she tried to apply makeup.

"Adara, you look great," he reassured her, even though her lips were bloodless and her eyes pools of anxiety.

Coming back from a place of dark thoughts, she gripped his forearm with a clammy hand. "Thank you for being here with me. I don't know if I could have done this alone."

Shaken by the reliance and trust her statement represented, he wanted to pull her into his arms and assure her he'd always be here, but she was already pulling away from him. She had been waiting for this a long time and he could see she was both eager and filled with trepidation. Not knowing her brother or how this would go for her filled him with his own anxiety, wanting to shield her yet knowing he had to let whatever happened happen. He could only accompany her outside where the sound of the chopper blades faded to desultory pulses.

Walking out a side door, they stood on the steps, Adara's fingernails digging into his biceps as she gripped his arm.

They watched Nic Marcussen help a woman with crutches from the helicopter. Rowan Davidson was vaguely familiar to him as a moderately famous child actress who'd had a flirtation with notoriety among the euro-trash social elite. She seemed surprisingly down to earth now as she spun with lithe grace on one foot, accepting her second crutch while trying to take a bag from her husband at the same time.

Nic shouldered the bag's strap and reached back

into the chopper for one more thing: an infant carrier.

As the couple made their way across the lawn toward them, Gideon felt the slicing gaze of the media magnate take his measure.

It wasn't often that Gideon met a man he considered his equal. Standing on the man's stoop didn't exactly put him on an even playing field and he might have been more uncomfortable with that if a severe expression of anguish hadn't twisted Nic's expression when he transferred his gaze to Adara.

Her tense profile barely contained the emotions Gideon sensed rising off her as viscerally as if they were his own. Everything in him wanted to pull her close and screen her from what was obviously a very painful moment. But he had to stand helplessly waiting out the silence as Nic paused at the bottom of the steps and the siblings were held in a type of stasis, staring at each other.

Like a burst of rainbows into a rainy afternoon, Rowan smiled and stepped forward. "We're so glad you came," she said in a warm Irish accent. Hitching up the steps on her crutches, she embraced Adara with one arm, kissing her cheek.

"I'm Rowan. It's my fault we're late. And you're Gideon?"

She hopped over to hug him as if they were long-lost relatives, and for once Gideon didn't take offense at an unexpected familiarity, accepting her kiss on his cheek, still focused on his wife who seemed to be in a kind of trance.

Slowly Nic set down the baby carrier and let the bag slide off his shoulder on his other side. He took a step forward and Adara tipped forward off the stoop, landing in the open arms of her brother. It was beautiful and heartrending, the reunion so intense it could only be the result of long, intense suffering apart.

"We should give them a minute," Rowan said huskily, her eyes visibly wet as she dragged her gaze from the pair. "Would you be an absolute hero and bring Evie into the house for me?"

Gideon didn't like leaving Adara, but followed Rowan to the kitchen where she began preparing a bottle. The baby craned her neck and followed Rowan with her Oriental eyes, beginning to strain against the confines of her seat, whimpering with impatience.

"I know, you're completely out of sorts, aren't

you?" Rowan murmured as she released the baby while the bottle warmed. Cuddling the infant, she nuzzled her cheek and patted her back, soothing the fussing girl.

"We were supposed to be here all summer just enjoying being a family," she said to Gideon. "Then it came up that I could have a few pins taken out of my leg. I wanted to put it off, but Nic said no, he could handle Evie for a couple of nights while I was in hospital. But Evie decided to cut a tooth and bellow nonstop. He didn't get a wink of sleep. Then he found out Adara had come looking for him. He didn't know which way to turn. Here, do you mind?" she said as a *ping* sounded from the cylindrical bottle warmer.

She held out the infant and Gideon had no choice but to take her so Rowan could retrieve the baby's bottle.

He held the sturdy little girl's rib cage between his palms. Her dangling legs wriggled and her tiny hands scratch-tickled his forearms while her doll's face craned to keep Rowan in view. She was the smallest, most fragile creature he'd ever held and fear that he'd break her made him want to hurriedly hand her back, but Rowan was occupied tipping the bottle to spray milk on her wrist then licking it off.

"I've used crutches so many times I can do a full tea service on them without spilling, but I haven't mastered juggling a baby. Yet." She smiled cheekily and hopped over to him. "Just rest her in the crook of your arm and—yes, I know you want that. You're hungry, aren't you? Uncle's going to feed you."

*No, I'm not,* Gideon thought, but found himself with a weight of soft warmth snuggled onto his forearm. As little Evie got the nipple in her mouth and relaxed, he did too. Her charcoal eyes gazed up at him trustingly and he felt a tug near his heart. Her foot tapped lightly onto his breastbone while she swallowed and breathed heavily with audible greediness. He felt like a superhero, making sure she wasn't going hungry.

"Shall we sit outside? I hope you've been comfortable here?" Rowan led him out of the kitchen to the patio.

"Very," he assured her, sincere. "You'll have to let us return the hospitality when our cruise ship launches next year. Now, how do we do this? Do you want to sit and take her—?"

A noise inside the house snapped Rowan's head around like a guard dog hearing a footstep. "That was Adara into the ladies' room. I'll just— Do you mind? I want to make sure Nic…" She *was* good on crutches, swooping away like a gull, a telling thread of concern in her tone as she disappeared into the house.

He snorted in bemusement, thinking that Nic Marcussen seemed the least likely man in the universe to require a mother hen for a wife, but apparently he had one.

While Gideon was literally left holding the baby.

He looked down at the girl, surprised to see how much of the bottle she'd drained. As her bright gaze caught his, Evie broke away from the teat to give him an ear-to-ear milky grin of joy and gratitude and trust.

A laugh curled upward from deep in his chest, surprising him with how instant and genuine his humor was. Little minx. They learned early how to disarm a man, didn't they? He was in very real danger of falling in love at first sight.

Adara wiped at her still-leaking eyes and tried to pull herself together so Gideon wouldn't worry.

He had been right. It was okay. Nico was and always had been her big brother in every way that counted. Nevertheless, her heart was cracking open under the pressure of deep feeling. She desperately craved the arms of her husband to cushion her from the sensation of rawness.

As she went in search of him outside, she saw him settling into a chair at the patio table, his back to her. Biting her lips together, she tried not to burst into happy tears as she stepped through the door and moved to his side—

—where she found him holding a baby, smiling indulgently at the infant as if the tot was the most precious thing in the world.

The kick of pain blindsided her. For a second she was paralyzed by the crash back to the reality of their imperfect life, winded so much she wasn't able to move, let alone retreat, before Gideon glanced up and saw the devastated expression on her face.

If he'd been caught with Lexi in flagrante delicto, he couldn't have looked more culpable. *It wouldn't have hurt this badly.*

"She's on crutches. The baby was hungry. I couldn't say no," he defended quickly while his arm moved in the most subtly protective way to draw the baby closer to his chest. In the way of a natural father sheltering his young.

At the same time, his free hand shot out to take Adara's arm in an unbreakable grip.

"You look like you're going to fall down. Sit." He half rose, used one foot to angle a chair for her and maneuvered her into it.

Adara's legs gave out as she sank into the chair. She buried her face in her hands and frantically reminded herself that her emotions were pushed to the very edge of endurance right now. The bigger picture here wasn't that he was stealing an opportunity to cuddle a baby because she couldn't give him one. He was getting to know their niece.

Longing rose in her as she made that connection and a different, more tender kind of emotion filled her, sweet with the layers of reunion with family that had driven her here in the first place. She lifted her head and held out her hands.

"Can I hold her? Please?"

"Of course." He transferred the baby's weight into her arms and Adara nearly dissolved into a puddle of maternal love. "Her name's Evie. Adara, I wasn't—"

She shook her head.

His hand came up to the side of her neck, trapping her hair against her nape as he forced her to look at him and said in a fierce whisper. "I wasn't trying to hurt you."

"I know. It's okay," she assured him, rubbing her cheek on the hardness of his wrist. "I just wasn't expecting it, that's all. I'm not mad."

He cupped the side of her face and leaned across to kiss her once, hard. "You scared me. I thought I was going to lose you."

She had to consciously remember to hold on to the baby while her limbs softened and her heart shifted in her chest. Every time she thought they didn't have a hope in the world of making something of their marriage, he said something like that and completely enchanted her.

Voices made them break their intense stare into each other's eyes.

"I'm not being a grouch," her brother growled as he emerged from the house carrying his wife in the cradle of his arms. "But you were discharged early because you promised to keep it elevated, so I think you should do that, don't you?"

Gideon moved to pull out a chair so Rowan

could slide down onto it, then he offered a hand to Nico. "Gideon."

"Nic," her brother said, completely pulled together after his tearful reassurances to her a few minutes ago. He'd never stopped caring or worrying about her all this time, just as she had for him. She was loved, was worth loving. It was a startling adjustment, like learning she wasn't an ugly duckling but a full-fledged swan.

Could Gideon see the change in her?

He wore a mask of subtle tension as he took his seat. No one else seemed to notice. Nic opened wine and Rowan stole the empty bottle of milk from her baby and handed Adara a burping towel.

When Nic set a glass of sparkling white before her, he smiled indulgently at Adara's attempt to pat a belch out of his daughter. "Looks like you know what you're doing. Do you have children?"

The canyon of inadequacy yawned before her, but Gideon squeezed her thigh and spoke with a neutrality she couldn't manage. "We've tried," he said simply. "It hasn't worked out."

"I'm sorry," Nic said with a grimace that spoke of a man wanting to kick himself for saying the wrong thing, but he couldn't have known.

"Not being able to get pregnant seemed like a horrible tragedy for me at first," Rowan said conversationally. "But we wouldn't have Evie otherwise and we can't imagine life without her. We're so smitten, we're like the only two people to ever have a baby, aren't we, Nic?"

"It's true," he admitted unabashedly while he settled into his own chair and absently eased Rowan's bandaged leg to balance across his thigh. His hand caressed her ankle, their body language speaking of utter relaxation and familiarity with each other. "I don't know what I did to deserve such good fortune."

The fierce look of deep love he gave his wife and the tender way she returned it was almost too intimate to witness, but Adara found herself holding her breath as yearning filled her. *I want that,* she thought, but even though she felt Gideon's fingers circle tenderly on the inside of her knee, she didn't imagine for a minute she'd get it.

The penthouse seemed cavernous and chilly when they returned from Greece. It was after midnight when they arrived after what had been a long, quiet flight.

They'd been through a lot since meeting up at the end of her brother's driveway, so she supposed it was natural they'd both withdraw a bit to digest it all, but the hint of tension and reserve Gideon was wearing bothered her.

They'd made love in the middle of the night and again first thing this morning. It had been wonderful as ever, but afterward, as they'd soaped each other in the shower, things had taken this turn into a brick wall.

Unable to get Gideon's look of paternal tenderness toward Evie out of her mind, she'd pointed out how her brother and his wife made adoption look like the most natural thing in the world.

"They do," he had agreed without inflection.

"It's something to think about," she had pressed ever so lightly. "Isn't it?"

"Perhaps."

So noncommittal.

Adara chewed her lip, completely open to the idea herself, but that meant staying married. Forever. To a man who didn't appear as enthused by the idea of children as she was.

He was such an enigma. Returning to New York was a cold plunge into her old marriage to a workaholic who liked his space and only communicated when he had to—if the scene she entered when she left the powder room was anything to go by.

Paul, their chauffeur, was exiting Adara's room where he would have left her luggage. Gideon was coming back to the living room from his own room, where he would have left his own. He swept his thumb across his smart phone as he gave Paul a rough schedule for the next few days, asking her absently, "Are you leaving early for the office with me tomorrow or do you want Paul to come back for you?"

Back to separate lives that revolved around their careers. She looked at her empty arms as she crossed them over her aching chest. "How early is early?"

He grimaced at the clock. "Six? The time change will have me up anyway."

Her too. "That's fine," she said, then thought, *Welcome back, Mrs. Complacent.* She'd obviously forgotten her spine back in Greece.

Paul wished them a good night and left. Gideon came across to set the security panel, then looked down at her as she stifled a yawn.

"Straight to bed?" he asked.

A bristling sensation lifted in the region between her shoulder blades and the back of her neck. His question was one of the shorthand signals they'd developed in this detached marriage of theirs. He was letting her off the hook for sex.

She was exhausted. It shouldn't bother her, but it left her feeling abandoned and without hope for their marriage, a family, or a love like her brother had found.

"Yes," she said quietly, pulling on her cloak of polite endurance to hide how hurt she was. "It's been a long day and tomorrow will be longer." Smooth out all those rough edges, Adara. Make it seem as if you don't have a heart to break.

"Your place or mine?"

"I—what?" She blinked at him, trying to quell the flutter of sensual excitement that woke in her blood. A little embarrassed by how quickly she could bloom back to life, she murmured, "I'm genuinely tired."

Nevertheless, she seesawed with indecision, longing for the closeness she experienced in his arms, but fearful of how neglected she felt when he drew himself apart from her the way he had since meeting her brother.

"I'm freaking exhausted," he admitted with heartfelt weariness, "but we're not going back to separate bedrooms. Mine," he said decisively, catching her hand to lead her there. "Don't bother moving your clothes. The farther away the better."

"Gideon." She chuckled a little as she stumbled behind him, then was distracted by entering a room she'd rarely peeked into. It was scrupulously clean and not just from the housekeeper doing a thorough job in their absence. Gideon was a tidy man. Living on boats forged that habit, he'd told her once. He didn't like clutter. The decorator's palette for the walls was unmarred by paintings or photos. The night table held only a phone dock that doubled as a bedside light.

He stepped into his closet to set his shoes on a shelf.

"You need to find a few days in the next week to come to Valparaiso with me," he told her as he emerged, drawing his belt free as he spoke, then hanging it precisely alongside the rest.

"You've become very dictatorial in the last few days, do you realize that?" She wasn't sure where the cheeky comment came from, but it blurted out even as her voice tightened along with her blood vessels. He was undressing, shedding his shirt without reserve to expose tanned planes of muscle.

"You used to be a pushover. I didn't have to try very hard to get what I wanted. Now I do."

"Does that bother you?" A pang in her lip made her realize she was biting down as she awaited his answer, habitually fearful of masculine disapproval.

He moved toward her, pants open to expose the narrow line of hair descending from his navel, feet bare, predatory with his tight abs and naked chest and sober expression. His nipples were pulled into tight points by the air-conditioned room.

She tensed against a rush of uncertainty and sexual admiration.

"You were thinking of leaving me because you weren't getting what you wanted. That bothers me very much." He cupped the side of her neck and his thumb pressed under her chin, gently tilting her face up. "We can't meet each other's needs if we don't say what they are, so I'm pleased you're telling me what you want. I'm telling you what I want. I like feeling you next to me and waking up to make love to you in the middle of the night. I need to travel and when I do, I want you to know that no one is in my bed except you."

So he hadn't completely left her, this man who so easily found his way to the deepest recesses of her soul. She swept her lashes down to hide how moved she was.

"What do you want, Adara?"

She practically liquefied into one of those women she often saw following him with limpid eyes and undisguised yearning. Her heart was so scarred and scared she could barely acknowledge what she wanted, let alone articulate it, but she managed to say huskily, "You."

Instantly it felt like too huge an admission, like she was confessing to a deeper need than the sexual ones he had. Unable to bear being so completely defenseless against him, she splayed her hands on his chest and tried to lessen the depth of the admission by saying in a stilted murmur, "I'm not a sexual person, but I want to be in bed with you *all the time.*"

Something inscrutable flashed in his expression, quickly masked by excitement as his chest expanded under her touch with a big inhale.

Adara hid her sensitivity in a sexual advance she couldn't have made a week ago, but their constant lovemaking over the last few days had given her the confidence to lean forward and tease his nipple with her mouth.

He grasped a handful of her hair while his erection grew against her stomach, making her smile as she flicked with her tongue and made him groan with approval.

"I thought you wanted to sleep," he said through his teeth.

"We will," she said, scraping her teeth across to his other nipple. "In a bit."

Gideon checked inside the velvet clamshell box, giving the ring one more critical look. The cushion-cut pink diamond was framed on either side by half-carat white diamonds, two on each side. Like Adara, the arrangement had a quiet elegance that wasn't ostentatious or flashy. It was a rare find that held the eye a long time once you noticed it.

When he'd seen it, he'd thought, *Sunrise. A new beginning.* Then his sailor's superstition had kicked in. *Red sky in morning...*

No, there was no warning here. They were

proceeding into the horizon on smooth waters, making this ring the perfect marker for their anniversary in a few weeks. He had considered waiting until the actual date to give this to her, but they had a gala tonight and it seemed the right time for Adara to show off a trinket from her husband.

A good time for him to show *her* off, he admitted to himself with a self-deprecating smirk. A funny pang hit him in the middle of his chest as he tucked the box into the pocket of his tuxedo jacket. Adara was the last person to walk around bragging, *Look what my husband gave me.* He was the one who'd coaxed her into accepting this invitation so he'd have an excuse to give her this ring and seal a deal they hadn't quite closed.

Moving into the empty living room to wait for her, he poured himself a drink and gazed at the lights bobbing across the harbor, disturbed by how insecure he still felt about their future.

If sex was an indicator, he had nothing to worry about. Horny as he may have been as a teenager, he hadn't had access to a female body often enough to be this sexually active. Since Greece, however, he and Adara had been living the sort of second honeymoon every man fantasized about. There shouldn't be an ounce of need left in him, but as he dwelled on waking this morning to Adara's curves melded into his side, and the welcoming moan she'd released when he'd slipped inside her, a flame of sexual hunger came alive in him again.

And it was so good. Not just the quantity, but the quality. Her old inhibitions were gone. She was outspoken enough that he could unleash himself with the knowledge that she'd slow him down if she didn't like it. The sex was a dream come true.

So he didn't understand this agitation in himself, especially when she'd become more open in other ways, making him feel even more special and privileged to wear the label "Adara's husband."

Like yesterday, when he'd swung by her office on impulse at lunch, catching her in a meeting. Through the glass wall he'd watched her hold court, standing at the head of a board table surrounded by men and women in suits, all glued to her words. He'd understood their fascination, hypnotized himself by the glow of—hell, it looked like happiness, damn it.

Adara had paused in sketching diagrams on a smart board to point the tip of her electronic pen at each person as she went round the table, soliciting comments, earning nods and building consensus.

Gideon had stood there transfixed, proud, awed, full of admiration while remaining male enough to enjoy the way her shirt buttons strained across her breasts, just a shade tighter than she used to wear them.

Maybe that wasn't entirely voluntary. She'd said something the other day about eating too much and being too sedentary while they were away. He'd dismissed the comment because who gained ten pounds in less than a week? And even if she had, he was quite happy with her curves, thanks. Studying that ready-to-pop button, he'd been torn between intense desire and the sheer pleasure of watching her work.

She'd turned her head and a flush of pleasure had lit up her expression. She'd bit back a smile, mouthing something about "my husband" to the crowd that turned their heads to the window.

He'd been busted and had to meet a pile of names he'd never remember. It had been worth it. Ten minutes later they had locked lips in the descending elevator and wound up doing a "snap inspection" on the family suite at one of her hotels, skipping lunch altogether.

It was all good. She'd even let him listen in to her calls to her younger brothers when she'd broken the news about looking up Nic. A few beseeching, helpless looks at Gideon while she walked through some difficult memories had kept him close, rubbing her back as she choked through the conversations, but afterward there'd been a level of peace in her that told him she was healing old wounds that had festered for years.

Tell her *your* secret, a voice whispered insidiously in his head.

He slipped his hand into his pocket to close his fist on the velvet box. *No.* It wasn't necessary. They were doing great. Her brother was on the other side of the world, not questioning where Adara's husband had come from. Gideon had dodged any curiosity from that quarter and there was no use rocking the boat.

Even though guilt ate him alive at the way Adara couldn't seem to get enough of watching her niece over the webcam. But what could he say? *Yes, let's allow strangers to dig into my past so we can adopt a baby*?

She hadn't brought it up again, but she didn't need to. It was obvious what she wanted and he couldn't do it.

Assaulted by a fresh bout of shame and remorse, he ducked it by glancing at his watch. It wasn't like Adara to keep him waiting.

Moving to her room where the bulk of her clothes and toiletries remained while their architect prepared renovation plans for a new master bedroom, Gideon was aware of a fleeting apprehension. He rarely checked in on her while she was getting ready. There was something about watching a woman put on makeup and dress to go out that triggered old feelings of being abandoned and helpless. He shook off the dark mood that seemed so determined to overtake him tonight, and knocked before letting himself into her room.

She was a vision of sexy dishevelment in a blue gown not yet zipped up her back. Her hair had ruffled from its valentine frame around her face, curling in soft scrolls around her bare shoulders while her flawless makeup gave her lips a sensual glow and added dramatic impact to the distempered expression in her eyes.

"Problem?" he asked, noting the splashes of

color where gowns had been discarded over the chair, the bed, and even the floor. Perhaps they should rethink the room sharing. This kind of disorder could wear on him.

"I told you we were eating out too much. I look like a lumpy sausage in every one of these. This one won't even close and my makeup doesn't match…" She was whipping herself into quite a state.

He bit back a smile, aware that he'd be on the end of a swift set down if he revealed how cute and refreshing he thought this tantrum was.

"Maybe the zipper is just caught. Let me try."

"It's not caught. I'm getting fat." She stood still as he tried to draw the back panels of the silk together and work the zipper upward. *Oh, hell.* This wasn't just a snagged zip, and now he'd done it: put himself in the position of having to acknowledge to his wife that she had gained a pound or two. Might as well go up to the roof and jump right now.

"See?" she wailed when he kept trying to drag the zip upward.

"Honestly, I don't see any weight gain," he insisted while privately acknowledging that spending as much time as he did caressing this body, a small and gradual gain would go completely unnoticed. "You're probably just getting your period. Don't women feel puffy then? You must be due for one."

Even as he said it, he was caught by the realization that she hadn't had one since, well, it would have been before they'd become intimate in Greece. At least a month ago.

He bristled with an unwelcome thought that he dismissed before it fully formed.

While Adara stood very, very still, her color draining away in increments.

Instinctively, Gideon took hold of her arm, aware of the way she tensed under his touch, as if she wanted to reject it.

"I, um, never get back to normal right away after a miscarriage," she summed up briskly, not looking at him while her brow furrowed. Her arm jerked to remove his touch as she shrugged into a self-hug. "You're probably right. It's just a particularly bad case of PMS bloating."

Except she'd also mentioned a few days ago that her breasts were sore because her bra was too tight.

Or tender because of something else?

He could see where her mind was going and it scared him because he really would lose her if she fell pregnant again.

"I use a condom every time, Adara. Every time." He'd been meaning to book a vasectomy, as permanent protection, but hadn't been ready to take the necessary break from sex.

"I know," she said so quickly it was almost as though she was trying to shut down the conversation before the word could be said, but it was there, eating the color out of her so she was a bloodless ghost refusing to look at him.

"So I don't see how—"

"I'm sure it's impossible," she cut in crisply. "And I'd only be a couple of weeks, not starting to put on weight, but I won't be able to think straight until I'm sure." Peeling the delicate straps of her gown off her shoulders, she let it fall to the floor and stepped out of the circle of midnight blue. Her strapless green bra didn't match the yellow satin and lace across her buttocks, but it was a pretty sight anyway as she walked into the bathroom. "I think there's a leftover test in the cupboard..."

She closed him out, the quiet click of the door a

punch in the heart. He rubbed his clammy hands on his thighs, insisting to himself it was impossible.

Even though Adara thought it *was* possible.

And she wasn't happy about it.

How could she be?

Bracing his hands on the edges of the bathroom door, he listened for the flush and heard the sink run. Then, silence.

He ground his teeth, waiting.

Oh, to hell with it. He pushed in.

She'd pulled on an ivory robe and stood at the sink, a plastic stick in her hand. It quivered in her shaking grip.

He moved to look over her shoulder and saw the blue plus sign as clearly as she did. *Positive.*

# CHAPTER EIGHT

THE VOLUME OF emotions that detonated in Adara was more than she could cope with. Dark and huge as a mushroom cloud, the feelings scared her into falling back on old habits of trying to compress them back into the shallow grave of her heart.

"The test is old, maybe. Faulty," Gideon said behind her.

"It was the second one in the box from when I tested myself a few months ago." She threw the stick away and washed her hands, scrubbing them hard, then drying them roughly before she escaped the bathroom that was luxuriously cavernous, but way too small when her husband was in it with her.

And she was pregnant.

Again.

Shock was giving way to those unidentified emotions putting pressure on her eyes and rib cage and heart. She didn't want him watching as they took her over and she had to face that *it was happening again.*

"You should go," she said briskly, keeping her back to him. "Make my apologies. Tell people I came down with the flu or something." She was distantly aware of the cold, slippery satin on her arms bunching under her fists, her whole being focused on listening for Gideon's footsteps to leave the room the way she was silently pleading for him to do.

"You're kidding, right?"

"I'm not in the mood to go out right now," she said sharply, grasping desperately for an even tone to hide how close she was to completely breaking down.

"Adara, I'm—"

"Don't you dare say you're sorry!" she whipped around to cry. Distantly she was aware of her control skidding out of reach, but the storm billowing to life inside her was beyond her ability to quell. "Maybe this is all the time we have with our children, but I won't be sorry they exist!"

Her closed fist came up against her trembling lips, trying to stem the flood that wanted to escape after her outburst.

"I'm not going anywhere," he said with quiet ferocity, moving toward her with what seemed like a wave of equally intense emotions swirling around him.

Their two force fields crackled with condensed energy as they met, heightening the strain between them. Adara looked into his face, really looked, and saw such a ravaged expression, such brutally contained anguish, her insides cracked and crumbled.

"Whatever happens, I'm staying right here." He pointed at the floor between their feet. "I won't leave you alone again. This is happening to *us*."

Emotion choked her then, overspilling the dam of denial to flood her with anguish and insecure hatred of this body that didn't know how to hang on to babies. Futile hope combined with learned despair to make her shake all over. She couldn't hold it back, had to say it.

"I'm scared, Gideon."

He closed his eyes in a flinch of excruciation. "I know," he choked out, and dragged her into his protective arms, locking her into the safety of a hard embrace. "I know, babe, I know."

It all came out in a swamping rush of jagged

tears. She clung hard to him as the devastating sorrow she'd never shown him was finally allowed to pour out of her. Every hurt that had ever scarred her seemed to rise and open and bleed free, gushing until it ran out the toxins, gradually closing in a seal that might actually heal this time.

As her senses came back to her, she realized he'd carried her to the bed where he'd sat down on the edge to cradle her in his lap. He gently rocked her, making comforting noises, stroking her soothingly.

"Sorry," she sniffed, wiping her sleeve across her soaked cheeks. "I didn't mean to lose it like that."

"Shh." He eased the edges of his jacket around her, cuddling her into a pocket of warmth close to his chest. When she looked up at him, she saw his eyes were red and glassy, his mouth twisted in frustrated pain.

"I wish—"

"I know. Me too." He steadied his lips in a flat line, the impact of his one sharp glance telling her he knew deeply and perfectly and exactly what she wished for.

When his hand moved into the folds of her

robe and settled low on her abdomen, she covered it with her own, willing their baby to know that Daddy was here too. Her heart stretched and ached.

Gideon swallowed loudly and drew in a heavy breath, things she felt viscerally with him as she rested her head against his heart. This is love, she thought. The knowing without words. The sharing of both joy and pain.

She sat in stillness a long time, wondering if it was true. Were they both here in this bubble of dawning heart-to-heart connection, or just her? Did he love her? A little?

Gideon swore softly and touched the pocket of his jacket. "Paul," he explained. "I should tell him we're not going. Is your phone in here?"

"On the dock in the living room."

"Here. You need to warm up." He dragged the covers back from the pillows before rising with her in his arms and neatly tucking her in.

Listless after her storm of weeping, Adara turned her back on his departure and let her eyes close and her mind go blank. She couldn't face that he'd walked out so dispassionately after holding her so tenderly.

She must have dozed because she woke still alone in the bed, but the bedside light was on and someone was rustling in her room. She opened her eyes to see Gideon fitting a hanger into one of her gowns and carrying it into the closet. A tiny smile dawned on her mouth as she surreptitiously watched him housekeep for her. He'd changed out of his tuxedo, which was always a pity because he made one look so good, but pajama pants were fine too. Even when they were obviously crisp and new from a package. Had he ever worn pajamas before tonight? she wondered.

His critical eye scanned the room for anything else out of place before he moved to the door.

Her heart fell. He wasn't going to join her. They were back to separate beds and separate lives.

But no. She heard the distant beep of him setting the alarm, then his footsteps padded back to her. He gently lifted the covers and eased into bed behind her.

She sighed and spooned herself into him.

"Did I wake you? I didn't mean to."

"It's okay. I won't be able to sleep anyway. I've already started thinking about doctor's appointments and taking vitamins and…" She sighed with heartfelt sadness. It seemed like such a futile effort to go through it all again. "…everything."

"I put in a call to Karen, letting her know we want an appointment tomorrow," he said, referring to her ob-gyn.

"Oh, um, thank you." His thoughtfulness startled her. She wouldn't have guessed that he even knew her doctor's name. Snugging herself a little more securely into him, she nuzzled the bent elbow beneath her cheek. "One less thing to worry about." Oddly, she found herself amused again. "Especially because you might actually get me an appointment tomorrow. I'd take whatever they offered, something next week if that's all they had, but no one says no to you, do they?"

"Not unless it's the answer I want to hear."

She snickered and turned in his arms. "Why are you like that?" she asked with sudden curiosity. "What made you so bullish?"

"Having nothing and hating it. You should get some sleep." He rolled back to reach for the light switch.

"Honestly, if I try to sleep, I'll just lie here and worry. Tell me something to distract me. What were you like as a child? Before your mom died," she prompted.

"Scared," he admitted, letting her glimpse the flash of angry honesty in his expression before he doused the light and drew her body into alignment with his. Her robe was bunched, her bra restrictive and the fabric of his pajama pants annoying when she wanted to stroke her bare leg on his.

At the same time, she was caught by the single word that didn't seem to fit with a mother he'd described as "maternal."

"Why were you scared?" she asked gently.

Gideon sighed. "I really don't like talking about it, Adara."

"Mmm," she murmured in old acquiescence, then said into his chest, "But I told you about my childhood, unhappy as it was, and we're closer for it. Aren't we?"

He sighed and rolled onto his back, arms loosening from his hold on her. "My story's a hell of a lot uglier than yours. I don't know much about my mother except what I told you before. I give her credit for somehow getting us into a rented room by the time she died, but before that, I can remember her leaving me in, literally, holes in the wall. Telling me to stay there until she came back. Can you imagine a woman—a child—trying to keep a baby alive while living on the street? I never felt safe."

"Oh, Gideon," she whispered, reaching her hand onto his chest.

He clasped her hand in his, taking care not to crush her fine bones, but was torn between rejecting her caress of comfort and clinging to it. He was sorry he'd started this, but part of him wanted to lay the groundwork. If his past ever came out, he wanted Adara to understand why he'd become who he was.

"I hate remembering how powerless I felt. So when you ask me why I go after what I want however I have to, that's why."

"How did she die?"

The unforgettable image of his mother's weary eyes staring lifelessly from her battered face flashed behind his closed eyes. He opened them to the streaks of moonlight on the bedroom ceiling, trying to dispel the memory.

"She was beaten to death." By a john, if he'd pieced things together in his mind correctly.

"Oh, my God! What happened? Did the police

find who did it? Where were you? Did you go into foster care after, or…?"

"I didn't stick around for police reports. I was so terrified, I just ran." All the way onto a ship bound for America, barely old enough to be in school.

"You *saw* her?"

"I told you it was ugly."

Her breath came in on a shaken sob. "I'm so sorry, Gideon. And you saw that other man, too. Your mentor."

"Kristor," he provided. Kristor Vozaras, but now wasn't the time to explain how they'd come to have the same name. "I knew I couldn't live like that, on the docks where crime is a career and a human life worth nothing. No matter what, I had to climb higher than carrying everything I owned in a bag on my shoulder. Whatever it took, I *had* to amass some wealth and take control of my destiny."

She moved her head on his chest, nodding in understanding perhaps. Her warm fingers stroked across his rib cage and she hugged herself tighter into him, the action warmly comforting despite his frozen core.

"I'm glad you didn't limit yourself," she said.

"I've always admired you for being a risk-taker. I've never had the nerve to step beyond my comfort zone."

"Oh, Adara," he groaned, heart aching in his chest as he weaved his fingers into hers. "You're the most courageous woman I know." How else could she stare down the probability of another heartbreak with fierce love for their child brimming in her heart?

Maybe he couldn't control whether or not she kept this baby, but he was going to fight like hell to keep her. *No matter what.*

Adara woke in her old bed and thought for a second it was all a dream. She hadn't gone to Greece, hadn't found closeness with her husband…

Then he padded into her room, half-naked, hair rumpled, expression sober as he indicated the phone in his hand. "Karen wants to know if we can get to her office before the rest of her patients start arriving."

It all came rushing back. *Pregnant.* Fear clutched her heart, but she ignored the familiar angst and sat up, nodding. "Of course. I'll get dressed and we can leave right away."

"Um." Gideon's mouth twitched. "You might want to wash your face."

Adara went to the mirror and saw a goth nightmare staring back at her. "Right," she said with appalled understatement.

Gideon confirmed with Karen and left for his own room to dress.

Their lighthearted start became somber as Gideon drove them to the clinic, neither of them speaking while he concentrated on the thickening traffic and the reality of their history with pregnancy closed in on them.

Nevertheless, as urgently as Adara wanted to self-protect right now, she also really, really appreciated Gideon's solid presence beside her. He warmed her with a strong arm across her back as they walked up to Karen's office and kept a supportive hold on her as they stood numbly waiting for the receptionist, still in her street jacket, to escort them into an exam room.

Karen, efficient and caring as she was, was not pleased to learn Adara had miscarried two months ago without telling her.

Adara drew in a defensive breath, but Gideon spoke before she could.

"Let's not dwell on that. Obviously there was no lasting damage or Adara wouldn't be pregnant again. I'd like to focus on what we can do to help her with this pregnancy."

Karen was used to being the one in charge, but shook off her ruffled feathers as Gideon's obvious concern shone through.

"I'd like to say there was a magic formula for going to term. Mother Nature sometimes has other plans, but we hope for the best, right? Adara, you know the drill." She handed her a plastic cup.

A few minutes later, Adara was in a gown, sitting on the edge of the exam table while Karen confirmed her pregnancy. The frown puckering her brow brought a worried crinkle to Adara's and Gideon's foreheads as well.

"What's wrong?" Adara asked with dread.

"Nothing. Just our tests are more sensitive than the over-the-counter ones and.... Do you mind? I won't do an internal just yet, but can I palpate your abdomen?"

Adara settled onto her back and Karen's fingers pressed a few times before she set the cool flat of the stethoscope against her skin. "Tell me more about this miscarriage you had. When do you think you conceived that time?"

"Um, late April?" Adara guessed. "I can look it up on my phone."

"So fourteen, maybe fifteen weeks ago?" The cool end of the stethoscope was covering a lot of real estate.

"You're not thinking I'm still pregnant from then," Adara scoffed. "Karen, I know a miscarriage when I'm having one."

"I want you to have a scan. Let's go down the hall."

Gideon's face was as tight as Adara's felt. He held her elbow, but she barely felt his touch, limbs going numb with dread. Something was wrong. Really wrong. Karen's sobriety told her that.

Except that, five minutes later, they were looking at a screen that showed an unmistakable profile of a baby's head, its tiny body lounging in a hammock-like curve, one tiny hand lifting above its head to splay like a wishing star.

Gideon cussed out a very base Greek curse. Not exactly appropriate for such a reverent moment, but Adara had to agree. This was unbelievable.

"Is that a recording from someone else?" she asked, afraid to trust her eyes.

"This is why we put you through those procedures during a miscarriage, Adara," Karen said gently. "We look for things like a twin that might have survived. Given that this one has hung on past your first trimester, I'd guess he or she is exactly that. A survivor. This is a very good sign you'll go to term."

# CHAPTER NINE

IF THEY'D WALLOWED in disbelief and shock last night, and tension had been thick on their way to see Karen, it was nothing to the stunned silence that carried them back to the penthouse.

Adara sank onto the sofa without removing her jacket or shoes, totally awash in a sea of incredulity. She was afraid to believe it. They might actually have a baby this time. A family.

An expansion of incredible elation, supreme joy, as if she had the biggest, best secret in the world growing inside her, was tempered by cautious old Adara who never quite believed good things could happen to her. She might have a solicitous husband who felt every bit as protective and parental toward his offspring as she did, but he wasn't in love with her. Not the way she was tumbling into love with him.

Shaken, she glanced to where he stood with hands in his pockets, the back of his shirt flattened by his tense stance, the curve of his buttocks lovingly shaped by black jeans, his feet spaced apart for a sailor's habitual seeking of balance.

"What are you thinking?" she invited hesitantly.

"That I can't believe I let you climb down to that beach in Greece. I've been on you like a damn caveman…" He ran a hand over his hair and turned around. His face was lined with self-recrimination. "I wish to hell I'd known, Adara."

She set her chin, not liking the streak of accusation in his tone. Sitting straighter, she said, "I'm not going to apologize for refusing to see a doctor before today." Even though a lot of things would have been different if she had.

Would she and Gideon have come this far as a couple, though?

And was this far enough?

She clenched her hands and pressed her tightened mouth against her crossed thumbs, trying to process how this pregnancy changed everything. While Gideon had shown no desire to discuss adoption, she had kept divorce on the table. Now…

"It's done anyway," he said, pacing a few steps, then pivoting to confront her. "But moving forward, we're taking better care of you. Both of you. I'll start by informing your brothers you'll be delegating your responsibilities. I want you working four-hour days, not twelve. Travel is curtailed for both of us. Chile will have to wait and Tokyo will go on hold indefinitely. The architect needs to start over and you can't be here through renovations, so we'll have to hurry the Hampton place along."

"Karen said everything is normal, that this isn't a high-risk pregnancy," she reminded, tensing at all he'd said. "I can still work."

"Do you want to take chances?"

"Of course not. But I don't want to be railroaded either. You're acting like—"

Imperious brows went up. "Like?"

"Like it's actually going to happen," she said in a small voice. She watched the toes of her shoes point together. All of her shrank inward, curling protectively around the tiny flicker of life inside her.

"You just said yourself, it's not high risk." His voice was gruff, but she heard the tiny fracture in his tone. He wasn't as steady as he appeared.

"It's just…to make all these changes and tell people…What if something happens?"

The line of his shoulders slumped. He came to sit beside her, angled on the cushion to face her while he pinched her cold fingers in a tight grip. "I'm going to move whatever mountains need moving to ensure nothing does. We're going to have this baby, Adara."

She didn't look convinced. Her brow stayed pleated in worry, her mouth tremulous. A very tentative ray of hope in her eyes remained firmly couched, not allowed to grow.

Gideon clenched his teeth in frustration that sheer will wasn't enough. "I realize you're scared," he allowed.

"I may not be high risk, but there's still a risk," she insisted defensively.

She was breaking his heart. "I'm not disregarding that. But my coping strategy is to reduce the chances of any outcome but the one I want and go full steam ahead."

"And the outcome you want is…a baby?"

"Is there any doubt?" He sat back, unable to fathom that she'd imagine anything else.

"I asked you what you were thinking and you started talking about architects and Tokyo, like this was a massive inconvenience to your jam-packed schedule."

His breath escaped raggedly. "I'm a man. My first thoughts are practical—secure food and shelter. I'm not going to hang my heart out there and admit to massive insecurities at not knowing how to be a father, or reveal that I'm dying of pride."

Her mouth twitched into a pleased smile. "Or own up to whether you'd prefer a boy or a girl?" Underlying her teasing tone was genuine distress. Adara would have had more value in her father's eyes if she'd been a male, they both knew that.

That wasn't why he took her question like a lightning rod to the soul, though, flinching then forcing his expression smooth. "I've always wanted a girl," he admitted, feeling very much as if his vital organs were clawed from him and set out on display. "So we could name her Delphi, for my mother."

Adara paled a bit and he knew he'd made a mistake. He could practically see her taking on responsibility for never giving him that.

"Babe—"

"It's a lovely name," she said with a strained, sweet smile. "I'd like it very much if we could do that."

But she wasn't like him, willing to bet on long shots. Her cheekbones stood out prominently as she distressed over whether she could come through for him. He didn't know how to reassure her that this wasn't up to her. He had never blamed her, never would.

"Will you wait here a minute?" He kissed her forehead and stood, leaving to retrieve the ring he'd wanted to give her last night. When he returned, he sat on the edge of the sofa again, then thought better and dipped onto one knee. "I bought this to mark our fifth anniversary, but…"

Adara couldn't help covering a gasp as he revealed the soft pink diamond pulsing like a heart stone of warmth from the frozen arrangement of white diamonds and glinting platinum setting.

"No matter what happens, we have each other." He fit the ring on her right hand.

Her fingers spasmed a bit, not quite rejecting the gift, but this seemed like a reaffirmation of vows. She had been prepared to throw their marriage away a few weeks ago and didn't know if she was completely ready to recommit to it, but she couldn't bring herself to voice her hesitations when her ears were still ringing with his words about his mother. Every time she'd lost a baby, his mother had died for him again. Small wonder he didn't wear his heart on his sleeve.

Given time, would it become more accessible?

He kissed her knuckles and when he looked into her eyes, his gaze was full of his typical stamp of authority, already viewing this as a done deal. The impact was more than she could bear.

Shielding her own gaze, she looked at his mouth as she leaned forward to kiss him lingeringly. "Thank you. I'll try to be less of a scaredy-cat if you could, perhaps, let me tell my mother before calling the architect?"

She glanced up to catch a flare of something in the backs of his flecked eyes that might have been disappointment or hurt, but he adopted her light tone as he said, "I'm capable of compromise. Don't drag your feet."

For a woman battling through an aggressive cancer treatment, as Adara's mother, Ellice, was, the quiet of Chatham in upstate New York was probably perfect. For a man used to a nonstop pace through sixteen-hour days, the place was a padded cell.

It's only one afternoon, Gideon chided himself. Adara had tried to come alone, but he had insisted on driving her. Still reeling over yesterday's news, he already saw that the duration of her pregnancy would be a struggle not to smother his wife while his instinct to hover over her revved to maximum.

Letting her out of his sight when they'd arrived here had been genuinely difficult, but he respected her wish to speak to her mother alone. She had yet to bring up the topic of Nic. Ellice had been too sick for that conversation, but with doctor reports that weren't exactly encouraging, Adara was facing not having many more conversations with her mother at all.

Scowling with dismay at the rotten hands life dealt, Gideon walked the grounds of the property that Adara's father had bought as an "investment." The old man had really been tucking his wife away from the city, isolating her as a form of punishment because he'd been that sort of man. Gideon saw that now. Not that it had been a complete waste of money. The land itself was nice.

Gideon wondered if either of Adara's brothers wanted this place when their mother passed. With only a dried-up pond for a water view, it wasn't

Gideon's style. He didn't need a rolling deck beneath his feet, but he did like a clear view to the horizon.

Maybe that was his old coping strategy rearing its head. Each time his world had fallen apart, he'd looked into the blue yonder and set a course for a fresh start. One thing he'd learned on the ocean: the world was big enough to run away from just about anything.

Not that he was willing to abandon the life he had here. Not now.

He stilled as he noticed a rabbit brazenly munching the lettuce in the garden. Bees were the only sound on the late-summer air, working the flowers that bordered the plot of tomatoes, beans and potatoes. The house stood above him on the hillock, white with fairy-tale gables and peaks. Below the wraparound veranda, the grounds rolled away in pastoral perfection.

It was a vision of the American dream and he was exactly like that invasive rabbit, feeding on what wasn't his.

His conscience had already been torturing him before Adara had turned up pregnant. Now all he could think was that he'd be lying about who he was to his son or daughter along with his wife.

But he couldn't go back and undo all the things he'd done to get here. He'd barely scratched the surface of his past when he'd told Adara he'd started working young. Child labor was what it had been, but as a stowaway discovered while the ship was out to sea, he could as easily have been thrown overboard.

Kristor had put him to work doing what a boy of six or seven could manage. He'd swabbed decks and scrubbed out the head. He'd learned to gut a fish and peel potatoes. Burly men had shouted and kicked him around like a dog at times, but he'd survived it all and had grown into a young man very much out for his own gain.

By the time he was tall enough to make a proper deckhand, Kristor was taking jobs on dodgy ships, determined to build his retirement nest egg. Gideon went along with him, asking no questions and taking the generous pay the shady captains offered. He wished he could say he had been naive and only following Kristor's lead, but his soul had been black as obsidian. He'd seen dollar signs, not moral boundaries.

The ugly end to Kristor's life had been a vision into his own future if he continued as a smuggler, though. Gideon had had much higher ambitions than that. He'd been stowing his pay, same as Kristor, but it wasn't enough for a clean break.

Posing as Kristor's son, however, and claiming the man's modest savings as an "inheritance" had put him on the solid ground he'd needed. Kristor hadn't had any family entitled to it. Yes, Gideon had broken several laws in claiming that money, even going to the extent of paying a large chunk to a back-alley dealer in the Philippines for American identification. It had been necessary in order to leave that life and begin a legitimate one.

Or so he'd convinced himself at the time. His viewpoint had been skewed to basic survival, not unlike Adara's obdurate attitude when he'd first caught up to her in Greece. He'd been cutting himself off from the pain of losing Kristor in exactly the way he'd fled onto Kristor's ship in the first place, running from the grief and horror of losing his mother.

He couldn't say he completely regretted becoming Gideon Vozaras. At sixteen—nineteen according to the fresh ink on his ID—he'd sunk every penny he had into a rusting sieve of a tugboat. He repaired it, ran it, licensed it out to another boatman and bought another. Seven years later, he leveraged his fleet of thirty to buy an ailing shipyard. When that started to show a profit, he established his first shipping route. He barely slept or ate, but people started to call him, rather than the other way around.

Fully accepted as an established business by then, he'd still possessed some of his less than stellar morals. When he was ready to expand and needed an injection of capital, he started with a man known to let his ego rule his investment decisions. Gideon had walked into the Makricosta headquarters wearing his best suit and had his salesman's patter ready. He'd been willing to say whatever he needed to get to the next level.

He'd been pulled up by an hourglass figure in a sweater set and pencil skirt, her heels modest yet fashionable, her black hair gathered in a clasp so the straight dark tresses fell like a plumb line down her spine. She turned around as he announced himself to the receptionist.

He was used to prompting a bit of eye-widening and a flush of awareness in a woman. If the receptionist gave him the flirty head tilt and smooth of a tendril of hair, he missed it. His mouth had dried and his skin had felt too tight.

Adara's serene expression had given nothing away, but even though her demeanor had been cool, his internal temperature had climbed. She had escorted him down the hall to her father's office, her polish and grace utterly fascinating and so completely out of his league he might as well still have had dirt under his nails and the stink of diesel on his skin.

Three lengthy meetings later, he had been shut down. Her father had refused and Gideon had mentally said goodbye to any excuse to see her again. No use asking her to dinner. By then he had her full background. Adara didn't date and was reputed to be holding on to her virginity until she married.

When she had unexpectedly asked to see him a few weeks later, he'd been surprised, curious and unaccountably hopeful. She'd shown up in a jade dress with an ivory jacket that had been sleek and cool and infuriatingly modest, not the sort of thing a woman wore if she was encouraging an afternoon tryst.

"I didn't expect to see you again," he'd said with an edge of frustration.

"I…" She'd seemed very briefly discomfited, then said with grave sincerity, "I have a proposal for you, which may persuade my father to change his mind, if you're still interested in having him as a backer. May I have ten minutes of your time?"

Behind the closed doors of his office, she had laid out what was, indeed, a proposal. She had done her homework. She had information on his financials and future projects that weren't public knowledge.

"I apologize for that. I don't intend to make a habit of it."

"Of what?" he'd asked. "Snooping into my business or running background checks on prospective grooms?"

"Well, both," she'd said with a guileless look. "If you say yes."

He'd been self-serving enough to go along with the plan. The upside had been too good, offering access to her business and social circles along with a leap in his standing on the financial pages. And Adara had made it so easy. She had not only scripted their engagement and wedding, she'd known her lines. Their marriage had been perfect.

To the untrained eye.

He could look back now and see what a performance it had been on both their parts. From the reception to country clubs to rubbing shoulders with international bankers, they had set each other up like improv specialists, him feeding Adara lines and her staying on message.

And she'd conformed to brand like a pro, elevating her modest style to a timeless sophistication that had put both the hotels and his shipyard in a new class. She'd delivered exactly what she'd promised in terms of networking, opportunities and sheer hard work, putting in the late hours to attain the goals he'd laid out.

She had probably thought that's all he'd wanted from her, he realized, heart clenching. It had been, initially, but somewhere along the line he'd begun to care—about a lot of things. She was an excellent cook and she bought him shirts he liked. Whenever they were about to leave for work or an evening event, she invariably smoothed his hair or straightened his tie and said, "You look nice."

Part of him had stood back and called her actions patronizing, but a needier part had soaked up her approval. It was all the more powerful because he had admired her so much.

Adara set a very high standard for herself. Once he'd fully absorbed that, he'd begun taking it as a challenge to meet and exceed her expectations. Finally comfortable financially, he'd followed her lead and started helping others, selecting charities with thought for who he really wanted to help, creating foundations that benefited young mothers, street kids, and sailors unable to work due to disabilities.

Meanwhile, pride of possession had evolved into something so deep, Adara's seeming to cheat on him earlier this summer had shaken him to the bone.

It wasn't comfortable to be this invested. Sure he was a risk-taker, but not with his emotions. The way his heart had grown inordinately soft, especially in the last weeks, unnerved him, but he couldn't help the way his chest swelled with feeling and pride every time he so much as thought about his wife.

A screen door creaked, drawing his glance.

Pressure filled his chest as Adara appeared on the veranda and lifted a somber hand.

He didn't deserve her or any of this, but he'd do anything to keep it.

Adara's emotions were all over the place and that look of intense determination on Gideon's face as he looked up at her gave her a chill near her heart. He seemed so ruthless in that second, exactly as her mother had just accused him of being. She could clearly see the man who'd said, *Whatever it took, I had to amass some wealth and take control over my destiny.*

But maybe her vision was colored by everything she was dealing with. When she started down the stairs, he met her at the bottom, his scowl deepening as he took in her red, puffy eyes. His arm was tender as he crooked it around her and drew her into his solid presence.

"Pretty rough, huh?"

She began to shake. Until the last few weeks, she'd had to keep her sorrows or worries inside her where they ate like acid. Now she had Gideon. Her mother was so wrong about him. He wasn't cold and heartless like her father. Not at all.

"Can we stay out here a few minutes? I feel like I haven't had air in weeks." Not that the summer heat held much oxygen, but he obliged, ambling beside her as she took a turn around the pond. "This would have been a great place to grow up if my father had bought this earlier. And things had been different," she mused, imagining a swing set and a sandbox.

"If Nic had been your father's, you mean?"

Adara choked on a harsh laugh, voice breaking as she said, "Mom asked me if this baby was yours." Her hand moved to protectively cover their unborn child's ears. "What prospective grandmother has that as a first reaction?"

"*I* don't have any doubt he or she is mine," Gideon said with quiet resolution. "But even if you told me right now that it wasn't, I'd stay right here and work through it with you."

Adara checked her step, startled, thinking again, *whatever it took...* "You wouldn't be angry?"

"I'd be angry as hell, but I wouldn't take it out on you and the baby the way your father tortured you and your mother. I wouldn't push you out of my life to fend for yourself, either."

The way his mother had had to make her own

way. Adara's surprise and apprehension softened to understanding. He might have a streak of single-mindedness, but there was a marshmallow center under his hard shell.

"You're a bigger person than me. Maybe it's the miscarriages and fear of infidelity talking, but I don't know if I could stay married if you had a baby with someone else."

"You're not sure you want to stay married, as it is, and the only woman having my baby is *you*."

Adara pivoted away from that and continued walking, startled by the shaft of fear his light challenge pierced into her. It would seem her ability to dissemble around him was completely gone. He knew every thought in her head, every hesitation in her heart.

"My mother said she'd understand if it wasn't yours," Adara said with a sheared edge on her tone, recalling how that conversation had spun into directions she hadn't anticipated any better than this one. Holding on to her composure had been nearly impossible as her mother had tried to find parallels in their two lives. "My parents had had a fight and the engagement was off. That's why she slept with Nic's dad. Olief was a journalist flying

back to Europe. She had a layover. It was just a re-
bound thing. The sort of affair all her flight atten-
dant friends were having. Then my father called
and the wedding was back on."

"Even though she knew she was pregnant?"

"I guess paternity could have gone either way.
She loved my father so she married him and de-
luded herself into believing Nic was his."

*At least you're not in love with your husband.
I've always been proud of you for having that
much sense, but children are a mistake, Adara.
You have no idea how much power a man has over
you once babies enter the picture.*

Adara had recoiled from her mother's words,
finding it distasteful to be accused of having no
feelings for Gideon even though that had been her
goal for most of her marriage.

"I wanted her to be happy for us and she just
took off on a bitter rant about my father." Hearing her mother refer to her grandchild as a "mistake" had been the greatest blow of all. Her entire
childhood, void as it had been of parental pride
and joy, had crawled out from under the bed, grim
and dark and ready to swallow her.

"She's sick," Gideon reminded her.

"I know, but—" *But you lied to him,* she had wanted to say. Maybe her father wouldn't have twisted into such a cruel man if his wife had been honest from the start.

There was no use trying to change her mother at this point though. Challenging her, arguing and judging, were incredibly misplaced. Her mother wasn't just sick, she was dying.

"We'll do better by our child," Gideon vowed, pausing to turn her into him. He lifted her hand to graze his lips across the backs of her fingers. The ring he'd given her yesterday winked at her.

At the same time, his eyes held a somber rebuke. Gideon was a patient man, but this time he wasn't going to let her avoid his silent question. Even as she absorbed his earnest statement, her mother's voice whispered again, *You have no idea how much power a man has over you once babies enter the picture.*

But she wasn't her mother. There weren't any lies between her and Gideon. The secrets and recriminations that had surrounded her growing up, forcing her to close off her heart out of self-protection, were old news. Their child, unpolluted by any of that, gave her a chance to love cleanly and openly.

This fresh start with this man, who already stirred her so deeply, was a chance to build a truly happy life. If she dared believe she was entitled to it and opened herself to letting it happen. It was a huge leap of faith, but she'd taken one in marrying him at all. Maybe she was putting her heart at deep risk, but again and again he'd proven himself to be a man she could trust.

"We will, won't we?" she said in quiet promise.

Relief and a flicker of deeper emotion was quickly transformed into his predominant mask of arrogant confidence. For a second, he'd seemed moved, which made her heart trip, but now he was his typical conqueror self, nearly smug with triumph—which was familiar and oddly endearing, making her want to laugh and ignore her old self trying to warn her that she might be giving up too much too quickly.

But if she had a soupy, awed look on her face, he wore one of fierce tenderness.

"You're so beautiful." The kiss he bent to steal was as reverent and sweet as it was hard and possessive.

Her lips clung to his as he drew away.

"Don't get ideas," he chided, breaking contact from her look of invitation. "We're cut off until you deliver."

"That's you being overcautious. Karen didn't say we couldn't." She was still aggravated that they'd shared a bed last night but hadn't made love. She was nervous about doing anything to jeopardize her pregnancy, but they'd been making love without consequence until now.

"Karen doesn't know how insatiable we are once we get started. Just do me a favor and don't make this harder than it is."

"Pun intended?" She drifted her gaze down his front to the bulge behind his fly.

"This is going to be a very long pregnancy." He gritted his teeth, making her laugh as he guided her inside for an early dinner before driving home.

# CHAPTER TEN

AFTER YEARS OF being the one who micromanaged to ensure everything met her father's impossible standards, Adara was forced to let go and trust others to pull off top-notch work with minimal input. It wasn't easy, but she eased up and was pleasantly surprised by her very efficient teams. Despite her working from home for months, only checking in electronically, they were managing great things without her.

Staying away from the office had a drawback, however. Moving through the ballroom decorated in fall colors of gold, crimson and burnt umber, she couldn't help congratulating people on putting together a brilliant event to celebrate the Makricosta chain's thirty-fifth anniversary. They all reacted with great surprise and when Adara met up with Connie, a woman she'd worked closely with for years, she realized why.

Connie rocked back on her four-inch heels.

"Wow, I've never seen a woman as pregnant as you act so happy and outgoing. When I got that big, I was a complete cow."

"Oh, I…" Adara didn't know what to say. Had her personality been frozen for so many years that a bit of friendly warmth was remarkable? Or was she really as big as she felt?

"That's meant as a compliment," Connie rushed to say, glancing with horror at Adara's guardian angel, Gideon.

They'd learned to give each other space in the confines of the penthouse as they worked from home, but tonight he was right beside her, his ripped masculinity nearly bursting out of his tuxedo. He didn't complain about their abstinence nearly as much as she did, but he spent a lot of time expending sexual energy in the weight room. It showed, making his presence all the more electric, while Adara's insecurity ballooned to match her figure.

"It's true," he said with a disturbing slide of his hand beneath the fall of her hair. His touch settled in a light, caressing clasp on the back of her neck, making her follicles tighten. "The pregnancy glow isn't a myth. You're gorgeous."

"I look like the *Queen Mary*," Adara sputtered. Her reports from Karen continued to be good, and weight gain was to be expected, but playing dress-up for this evening hadn't been as fun as it used to be. Her hair had developed kinks, she was too puffy for her rings and wearing heels was out of the question. Growing shorter and pudgier while her husband grew hotter and sleeker was demoralizing. All her excitement in having a date night deflated.

"I only meant that you seem very happy. When are you due?" Connie prompted.

Adara couldn't help brightening at the topic of delivering a healthy baby, her misgivings from early in the pregnancy dispelled by her baby's regular jabs and the closing in of her due date. Nowadays her fears were the natural ones of any mother, most specifically that her water would break while she was in public.

But a few minutes later, when Gideon interjected, "We should start the dancing," and guided her toward the floor, her self-consciousness returned. He must have felt her tension. As he took her in his arms, he chided, "Are you genuinely worried about how you look? Because I was being sincere. You're stunning."

Biting off another self-deprecating remark, she chose to be truthful. "We haven't been going out much, so I guess I wasn't expecting so many stunned expressions at how huge I am. And look around, Gideon. Wait, don't. There are far too many women with teensy waistlines and long legs and—"

"None with breasts like yours. Do you think I've looked anywhere but down your dress tonight? Unless it's at your lips. You're not wearing lipstick, are you? That's all you, ripe and pouty and pink. You're sexy as hell."

Said lips parted in surprise. Everything seemed to taste funny these days, lipstick included, so she'd opted for a flavorless lip balm and yes, had noted that even her lips looked fat. She might have bit them together in an attempt to hide them, but his wolfish fixation on her mouth sent tendrils of delight through her.

With a little moue she said, "Really? You're not just saying that?"

With a low growl, he stopped dancing and claimed her mouth with his own.

The kiss was devastating, making her knees want to fold so he had to tighten his hold on her, shifting her to an angle to accommodate her bump. That tilted her head just enough to seal their lips with erotic perfection.

He didn't keep it to a quick punctuation to prove a point, either. Adara put up a hand to the side of his head, thinking, *People are watching,* but he gave her tongue a wicked tag and she couldn't help letting the kiss deepen and continue.

Oh, this man could kiss.

A cleared throat brought her back to reality with a *thunk* that she felt all the way into the flats of her feet. A woman's amused Irish lilt said, "Don't interrupt them. They're adorable."

"Nic," Adara breathed in recognition of her older brother and his wife, growing hot with embarrassment as she realized what a show they'd been putting on. "Hi, Rowan. It didn't sound like you'd make it."

Her brother and his wife were beyond star power, Nic in a tuxedo and Rowan showing off her lithe dancer's body with an off-the-shoulder figure-hugging green gown.

"Evie got over her cold and we wanted to see you again," Rowan said.

Nic leaned in to kiss Adara's cheek before he shook hands with Gideon.

Something passed between the two men that she couldn't quite interpret and didn't get a chance to study. Having kept up via webcam, she and Rowan had become tight friends and that gave them plenty to talk about. The rest of the evening passed in a blur of catching up while also going through the routine of photo ops and speeches for the anniversary celebration, partaking of the buffet, and finally returning to the penthouse exhausted but still keyed up.

"That went well, don't you think?" she asked Gideon as she removed her earrings. They were enchanting cascades of diamonds commissioned to match her ring. She'd almost ruined her makeup when he'd presented them to her before they'd left earlier in the evening, she was so affected by his thoughtfulness.

Gideon made a noncommittal noise.

"No?" she prompted, alarmed that he might have noticed a flaw she'd missed.

"Hmm? No, it was fine. Perfect. Excellent. I'm

a bit distracted. Look, you get ready for bed and I'll be in soon. I'd like a nightcap."

"Oh. Okay." Adara's startled confusion was evident, but Gideon didn't attempt to explain himself.

He breathed a small sigh of relief as she disappeared and didn't see the full measure of bracing whiskey he poured for himself or the rabid way he drained it. Despite the burn that promised forgetfulness, he wasn't able to stop replaying his conversation with her brother.

"I'd like a word," Nic had said when both their wives had been drawn across the room by some fashion marvel.

"Now is fine," Gideon had said, keeping one eye on Adara, premonition tightening his muscles.

"Understand first that I've always felt protective of Adara, even when the only thing she had to fear was a nightmare. Knowing what I abandoned her to, I'm sick with myself for not trying to contact her sooner. I'll be on guard for her the rest of my life."

"Reassuring," Gideon had muttered.

"The way you two were arguing at the end of my driveway wasn't," Nic retorted sharply. "When you first arrived in Greece. Not reassuring at all."

Gideon knew better than to show weakness, but he flinched involuntarily. "I thought she was meeting another man. Tell me how you would react if you thought your wife was stepping out on you."

"She wouldn't. But…" Nic shrugged, seeming to accept the explanation for Gideon's temper that day. "Regardless, I'm a man who collects the facts before he reacts."

Gideon had spilled a dry laugh at that point, enjoying the euphemistic phrase "collects the facts." "You mean you had me investigated."

"I don't have to hire people to do my legwork," Nic said disparagingly.

"No," Gideon snorted, wishing for a drink at that point. He'd known from the outset that Nic could be a threat, but he hadn't expected this. Not now when he and Adara had both found such happiness. "What did you learn?" He surreptitiously braced himself.

"What do you think I learned?" Nic asked, narrowing his eyes. "Nothing. Which doesn't surprise you, does it?"

"Of course it does," he'd lied. "I'm all over the internet."

"Gideon Vozaras is," Nic agreed. "He's never

made a wrong move. Some of his early business dealings weren't as clean as they could have been, but that's every scrappy young man trying to make his mark. Those men don't usually appear out of thin air, though."

Gideon had calmly stropped his knuckles on his jaw, trying to disguise that he was clenching his teeth. "I'm fairly protective of Adara myself, you know." He flashed a glance from her laughing face to the vague resemblance of her features in her brother's rigid expression.

The other man wasn't intimidated, but there was a watchful respect. He didn't take the danger of Gideon's temper lightly.

"I can see that things between you are different from the way they first appeared," Nic said. "But secrets destroyed my life. I won't let that happen to Adara."

"It's not secrets that destroy. It's the exposing of them. You really want to do that to her when she's found the first bit of happiness she's known since you were children?" He jerked his chin toward the circle of women where Adara was holding court with a flush of pleasure on her face, allowing another woman to feel the baby kick. "Think about what you're doing, Nic."

"No, you think about it," Nic had retorted sharply. "Do you want to make it easy and give me a name? Tell her yourself before I get there? Because I will."

"You want a name? Start with Delphi Parnassus and happy reading." He'd bit out the words and smoothly extricated his wife from the party, claiming she needed her rest.

"Gideon? Are you all right?" Adara asked him, yanking him back to the apartment where she stood in the bedroom doorway, face clean of makeup. Her hair was brushed into sleek waves. She wore one of his silk shirts, the front crossed over her bulging tummy and pinned by her folded arms. Her bump shortened the shirt, offering such a tantalizing view to the tops of her thighs, he reacted like a drug had been injected into his loins.

"Why are you wearing that?" His voice barely made it up from the depths of his chest.

"I've grown out of all my nightgowns," she said with aggravation. "Do you mind?"

"It's criminal, Adara," he admitted with a scrape in his throat, polishing the last of his drink. "We promised not to tease each other. Let me get you my robe."

She tilted her head to a skeptical angle as he brushed past her. "I wasn't trying to tease. But, be honest, are my legs okay? Because they seem swollen. No wonder everyone was appalled."

*Be honest,* echoed in his head, but the whiskey was burning through blood that had abstained from alcohol the way the rest of him had been going without his wife. Fear, genuine fear of losing her—not this penthouse or their cruise ship or the other properties they owned—edged out conscience or logic. All he wanted was to hold on to her. Tightly.

"It's been a long night. You should be asleep," he told her when she followed him into the bedroom.

"I had a nap before we left," she reminded, scowling as he shook out his robe and held it for her. "Does it strike you that we act less like a married couple these days than a nanny and her charge? You don't need to dress me."

He patiently continued to keep the robe suspended by the shoulders, inviting her to shrug her arms into the sleeves. "If I treat you like a child, it's only to remind myself that's why I can't have you. You know I'm crazy about you."

"But how could you be? Look at me!" She flashed open the shirt she'd been hugging over her front.

He shut his eyes, but not before he took a mental photograph of creamy skin, nipples dark and distended, lush, plump curves and a ripe round belly with an alluring shadow beneath that was *not* concealed by any satin or lace. She was naked and gloriously fertile.

This was why ancient men worshipped the goddess who provided their young.

"You can't even look!"

"For God's sake, Adara." He hung the robe on its hook and moved into his closet to change, needing the distance or he'd bend her over the nearest piece of furniture and *show* her how badly he wanted her. "If I wanted to sleep with a stick, I would have married one. You've always had a nice round ass and I like it. Frankly, it's better than ever in my opinion. See how hot I am for you?"

He paused in hanging his tuxedo pants over a rod and moved into the doorway, showing her his straining erection barely contained by his boxers.

Every cell in his body was primed for her and this fight was only shredding what little control he had left. It didn't help that he was also dealing with Nic's threats, feeling his grip on Adara and their life together slipping away. He wanted to cement their connection with a prolonged act of intimacy, but it wasn't possible.

Adara's gaze went liquid as she roamed it lovingly down his form, wetting her lips as she stared at the shape straining against the molding fabric of his shorts.

"I could—"

"I told you, we're in this together," he muttered, turning away from her offer even though it was like wrenching muscle tissue from his bones. But every time he thought of the way she'd gone down on him to protect this pregnancy in the first place, and that he'd resented not having all of her, he felt like the biggest heel alive.

He *was*.

He finished stowing his clothes and stepped into his pajama bottoms, returning to the bedroom to find her buttoning his shirt up her front, not looking at him.

He sighed, but what could he say?

A few seconds later, the lights were out and that delicious ass of hers was pressed firmly into his lap, driving him insane as she wiggled to get comfortable.

"Can I have your arm?" She lifted her head.

He obliged, sliding his arm under her neck the way she liked. As she settled and sighed, he smoothed her hair back from her ear and rested his lips against her nape. His other hand splayed on her belly and he let out a breath as well.

She was still tense though and it made it impossible for him to relax.

"Don't be angry," he cajoled. "This is only for a couple more months."

*"Months,"* Adara cried, nearly ready to burst into tears of frustration. Feeling his erection against her cheeks didn't help.

"Weeks," he hurried to say, even though they both knew it was eight.

"I'm dying." She covered his hand with hers and drew his fingers into contact with the wet valley between her thighs. "See?"

It was something she couldn't have even contemplated doing half a year ago, but they'd grown close and honest and sexual. Her body wasn't as visual as his when it came to showing how aroused she was, but she wanted him to know how badly she was suffering. She expected him to pull away and scold her, but he surprised her by burying a groan against her neck and stroking deeply and with more pressure. He explored her with the familiar expertise that always drove her directly to the edge.

Her hips rocked instinctively into his caress, then back into that teasing hardness behind the thin shield of fabric pressed against her bottom. His other arm shifted to clamp around her, clasping one full breast and caging her to the wall of his body while he bit her neck. His hips pushed against her and he pressed two fingertips where she felt it most, pinning her in a vise of sheer delight.

A quicksilver shiver was chased by a shudder and then the quaking poured through her, running like fire between her thighs and suffusing her whole body in sparkling waves of pleasure. The contractions were huge and stunning and incredible. She mindlessly prolonged them by grinding his hand between her legs and rocking her hips against his erection, loving everything about this wildly intimate act.

When the paroxysm receded, she gasped for a normal breath.

Gideon's caressing fingers left her. She protested with a little murmur. Her body wanted more and more and more, but a sweet lassitude filled her too. *Now* she felt sexy and adored.

She also realized her neck stung. Gideon had left a love bite there.

Dazed but determined to keep things equal between them, she tried to turn. He swore and rolled away.

"Don't be mad—" She realized there was also a wet patch on her back. Plucking at it, mind hardly able to comprehend how… "Did you—?"

"Yes," he said tightly. She sensed he was lifting his hips to remove his pajama pants. A second later the pants were dragged from beneath the covers and sent flying across the floor. "What the hell did you just do to me? I haven't done that since, hell, I don't think I've ever lost control like that. It's not funny."

Adara couldn't help the fit of giggles as she sat up to remove his shirt. "I was kinda caught up and didn't realize you were with me. That's nice. I'm glad."

"Yeah, I noticed you were enjoying it. That's why I was so turned on, but I didn't mean to lose it completely. Thank God it's dark. I'm so embarrassed—would you quit laughing?" He threw the stained shirt after the pants.

"I'm sorry," she said, unable to help convulsing with giggles as he spooned her into him again, skin to skin. It felt incredible and she snuggled deeper into the curve of his hot body. "Was it good for you?"

"What do you think? It was fantastic, you brat. How's baby? Did I hurt you? I was holding you pretty tight. Good thing you're not going anywhere tomorrow, with that giant hickey on your neck."

"We're fine. Both very happy." She smiled into the dark, melting as he caressed her belly and nuzzled her ear. "But you're not going to leave those clothes on the floor, are you?" she teased.

He stilled and let out a breath of exasperation. "They're fine till—oh, hell, it'll drive me crazy now you've said it and you know that, don't you?" He flung off the covers and gathered the shirt and pants to throw them in the hamper. "Enjoying yourself?" he asked as he returned to the bed that was shaking with her laughter.

Adara used the edge of the blanket to stifle her snickers. "I'm sorry. That was mean, wasn't it?"

"Yes, it was," he growled, cuddling her into him once more. They both relaxed. "But you must believe me now. About finding you irresistible?"

"I do," she agreed, sleepily caressing the back of his hand where it rested on the side of her belly. Tenderness filled her and she knew she'd never been this happy in her life. "And I can't help thinking... Gideon?"

"Mmm?" he responded sleepily.

"Are we falling in love?" Her heart stopped as she took that chance. It was such a walk straight off a cliff.

That didn't pay off.

Stillness transformed him into a rock behind her. Her postorgasmic relaxation dissipated, filling her with tension. His breath didn't even stir her hair.

Stupid, stupid, Adara. Hadn't she learned a millennium ago not to beg for affection?

"I'm not sure," he said in a gruff rasp.

"It was a silly question. Never mind. Let's just go to sleep. I'm tired." She resolutely shut her eyes and tried to force herself to go lax, to convince him she was sleeping, but she stayed awake a long time, a thick lump in her throat.

And when she woke in the night, he was no longer in the bed with her.

Gideon stood before the living room windows and saw nothing but his past. A dozen times or more over the years, he'd considered coming clean with Adara. Every time he'd talked himself out of telling her his real name, but this time he wasn't finding an easy way to rationalize keeping his secret.

At first it had been a no-brainer. She'd been all business with her proposal, selling him the upside of marriage in her sensible way. The hook had been deliciously baited with everything he'd ever wanted, including a sexy librarian-style wife. Telling her at that point that he was living under a false name would have deep-sixed their deal. Of course, he'd stayed silent.

His conscience had first pinched him the morning of their honeymoon though. She'd come to the breakfast table so fresh faced and shy, barely able to meet his gaze. He'd been incapable of forming thoughts or words, his entire being filled with excited pride as he recollected how trusting and sweetly responsive she'd been.

*"Any regrets?"* she'd asked into the silence, hands in her lap, breath subtly held.

*"None,"* he'd lied, because he'd had a small one. It had niggled that she was so obviously good and pristine and unquestioning. He'd soiled her in a way, marrying her under pretense.

He hadn't exactly been tortured by his lie, doing what he could to compensate, even forgetting for stretches at a time as they put on charity balls and cut ribbons on after-school clubs. He had let himself believe he really was Gideon Vozaras and Adara legally his wife. Life had been too easy for soul-searching and when the miscarriages had happened, well, things had grown too distant between them to even think of confessing.

Since Greece, however, the jabs to his conscience had grown more frequent and a lot sharper. Honesty had become a necessary pillar to their relationship, strengthening it as much as the physical intimacy. He respected her too much to be dishonest with her.

And he loved her too much to risk losing her.

*God, he loved her.* Last night when she'd asked

him about his feelings, he'd been struck dumb by how inadequate the word was when describing such an expansive emotion. He'd handled it all wrong, immediately falling into a pit of remorse because he was misrepresenting himself. He *had* to tell her.

And he would lose her when he did.

He could stand losing everything else. The inevitable scandal in the papers, the legal ramifications, the hit to his social standing and being dropped from his numerous boards of directors… None of that would be easy to take, but he'd endure it easily if Adara stood by him.

She wouldn't. Maybe she would stick by a man who came from a decent background, but once he really opened his can of worms and she saw the extent of his filthy start, she'd be understandably appalled. It would take a miracle for her to overlook it.

Yet he had no choice, not with Nic breathing down his neck.

His heart pumped cold, sluggish blood through his arteries as he waited like a man on death row, waited for the sound of footsteps and the call of his name.

* * *

Adara didn't bother trying to go back to bed when she woke at six. Swaddling herself in Gideon's robe, she went to find him, mind already churning with ways to gloss over her gaffe from last night. If she could have pretended it hadn't happened at all, she would have, but it was obvious she'd unsettled him. She'd have to say something.

She found him standing at the window in the living room, barefoot and shirtless, sweatpants slouched low on his hips. His hair was rumpled, his expression both ravaged and distracted when he turned at the sound of her footsteps.

He didn't say anything, just looked at her as if the greatest misery gripped him.

Her heart clutched. This was all her fault. She'd ruined everything.

"It was never part of our deal, I know that," she blurted, moving a few steps toward him only to be held off by his raised hand.

He might as well have planted that hand in the middle of her chest and shoved with all his considerable might, it was such a painfully final gesture of rejection.

"Our *deal*..." He ran his hand down his unshaven face. "You don't even know who you made that deal with, Adara. I shouldn't have taken it. It was wrong."

She gasped, cleaved in two by the implication he regretted their marriage and all that had come of it thus far. He couldn't mean it. No, this was about his childhood, she told herself, grasping for an explanation for this sudden rebuff. He'd confessed that before they married he'd had a low sense of self-worth. He blamed himself for his friend's death. He had probably convinced himself he wasn't worthy of being loved.

She knew how that felt, but he was so wrong.

"Gideon—" She moved toward him again.

He shook his head and walked away from her, standing at an angle so all she could see was his profile filled with self-loathing. A great weight slumped his bare shoulders.

She couldn't bear to see him hurting like this. "Gideon, please. I know I overstepped. We don't have to go into crisis."

"It's not *you* that's done anything. You're perfect. And I wouldn't do this if your brother hadn't threatened to do it for me," he said through gritted teeth, as if he was digging a bullet from his own flesh. "I would never hurt you if I had a choice. You know that, right?"

"Hurt me how? Which brother? What do you mean?"

"Nic. He's threatened to expose me to you, so I have no choice but to tell you myself."

His despair was so tangible, her hand unconsciously curled into the lapels of the robe, drawing it tightly over the place in her throat that suddenly felt sliced open and cold. She instinctively knew she didn't want to hear what he had to say, but forced herself to ask in a barely-there voice, "Tell me what?"

He solidified into a marble statue, inscrutable and still, his lips barely moving as he said, "That I'm not Gideon Vozaras."

After a long second, she reminded herself to blink, but she was still unable to comprehend. Her mind said, *Of course you are.* He wasn't making sense.

"I don't... What do you mean? Who is then?"

"No one. It's a made-up name."

"No, it's not." The refusal was automatic. How could his name be made up? He had a driver's license and a passport. Deeds to boats and properties. His name was on their marriage certificate. You couldn't falsify things like that. Could you?

She stared at him, ears ringing with the need to hear something from those firmly clamped lips, something that would contradict what he'd already said.

He only held her gaze with a deeply regretful look. His brow was furrowed and anguished.

No. She shook her head. This was just something he was saying to get out of feeling pressured to love her because...

Her mind couldn't conjure any sensible reason to go to this length of a tale to escape an emotional obligation. Rather, her thoughts leaped more quickly to the opposite: that it would make more sense to pretend to love in order to perpetuate a ruse. The nightly news was full of fraudsters who pretended to love someone so they could marry a fortune.

Her throat closed up and she took a step backward, recoiling from the direction her thoughts were taking. It wasn't possible. She was being paranoid.

But she couldn't escape the way tiny actions— especially those taken since she'd asked for a divorce—began to glow with significance. They landed on her with a weightless burn, clinging like fly ash.

*I fired Lexi.*

*I had self-worth because you gave it to me. People respected me.*

His sudden turn toward physical attentiveness and nonstop seduction. No baby wasn't a deal breaker, he'd said.

But adoption wasn't worth talking about *because that would require a thorough background check.*

Her heart shriveled and began to hurt. She brought a protective hand to her belly. He must have thought he'd won the lottery when she had turned up pregnant and their marriage was seemingly cemented forever.

*I wouldn't do this if your brother hadn't threatened to do it for me.*

He would have let her just keep on believing he was Gideon Vozaras.

"Who are you?" she asked in a thin voice, thinking, *This is a dream. A bad one.* "Where did Gideon Vozaras come from?"

He scowled. "I took Kristor's surname so I could pose as his son and collect what savings he had.

My first name came off the cover of a Bible in a hotel room." He jerked a shoulder, face twisting with dismay. "Sacrilegious, I know."

A fine tremor began to work through her and she realized she was cold. Too bad. There was no cuddling up to her husband for a warm hug. This man was a stranger.

The truth of that struck to her core.

"We're not married," she breathed. Somehow it was worse than all the rest. She was a good girl. Always had been. She'd saved herself for marriage. They'd had a wedding. Her father had finally approved of something she'd done. There were photos of them taking vows. All those witnesses had seen…a joke. A lie.

It was all a huge, huge lie.

Gideon—*the stranger*—flattened his mouth into a grim line. "In every way that matters, I am—"

"Oh my *God*," Adara cried, shaking now as her mind raced through all that this meant. He must have called his bookie and put everything he owned on a long shot when she turned up in his office asking to marry him. What a fantastic idiot she was! "You never loved me. You didn't even *want* me."

"Adara." His turn to take a step toward her and it was her turn to back away.

*Whatever it took, I had to amass some wealth...*

She remembered exactly how shocked he'd looked when she'd suggested marriage, how quick he'd been to seize the chance. How accommodating and willing to go with the flow of everything she asked, from waiting until the wedding night to keeping separate bedrooms.

She covered her mouth to hold back a scream. And last night she'd had to *beg* him to touch her. She'd had to plead because he'd been avoiding lovemaking—

Humiliation stung all the way to her soul.

"You've been laughing at me all this time, haven't you?" she accused as emotion welled in her. Hot, fierce emotion that made her tremble uncontrollably. "No wonder you fought so hard to stay married. Where would all of this go if we divorced?" She flung out an arm to encompass the penthouse and work space and high living they enjoyed. "Who would half of it go to? Thank God I was pregnant, huh, Gid—" She choked, aware she didn't even know his real name. "Whoever the hell you are."

Gideon's world was dissolving around him, but it had nothing to do with penthouses in the top of a tower. "Calm down," he said, grasping desperately at control, when he wanted to crush her to him and show her how wrong she was. "You're going to put yourself into labor. We can get through this, Adara. Look how far we've come since Greece."

It was a weakly thrown life ring, one that failed to reach her.

"How *far?*" she cried, rising to a new level of hysteria. "I thought we were learning to be *honest.* You might have mentioned this little secret of yours."

"I'm telling you now," he insisted.

"Because my brother extorted it out of you! If he hadn't, I'd still be in the dark, wouldn't I?"

He grappled for a reasonable tone, worried about the way her face was reddening. Her blood pressure wasn't a huge issue, but they were monitoring it. She'd complained of breathlessness a few times and her chest was heaving with agitation.

"We were happy," he defended.

"The mark is always happy when she's well and truly duped," she cried. "How could you do that to me? To anyone? What kind of man *are* you?"

She rushed him, looking as if she intended to pulverize him.

He caught her arms and held her off. He didn't care about his own safety. She could pummel him into the dirt if it made her feel better, but she and the baby were everything. If she didn't get hold of herself, she was going to hurt one or the other or both.

She struggled against his hold, but he easily used his superior strength to back her into the sofa, where he firmly plunked her into it, saying sternly, "Calm *down*."

"I have a criminal liar invading my home! I'm entitled to—oh, you bastard! I hate you." She tried to rise and strike at him. "How could you do this? How?"

He forced her back into the softness of the cushions. "You're giving me no choice but to walk out of here," he warned. "I'd rather stay and talk this out."

"And talk me round, you mean." She slapped at his touch. "Get out of here then, you scumbag."

The names didn't matter. The betrayal and loathing behind the words sliced him to the bone. He couldn't bear to leave her hating him like this, but even as he stood there hesitating, she was trying to rock herself out of the cushions and swipe at him at the same time, breasts heaving with exertion.

For her own safety, he couldn't stay. Every step to the door flayed a layer of skin from his body, but he moved away from her, waiting for a pause in her tirade of filthy names to say, "It was never my ability to love that was in question, Adara."

"You should have said it last night when I asked. I might have fallen for it then, but not now, you phony. Get out. And don't ever expect to see this child."

That was meant as a knife to the heart and it landed right on target, stealing his breath and almost taking him back into the fight, but as he glanced back, he could see how pale and fraught she was, obviously going into a kind of shock. He grabbed his cell phone on the way to the elevator and placed a call to Nic as the doors closed him out of his home.

"Get over here and make sure she doesn't lose our baby over this."

# CHAPTER ELEVEN

ADARA HAD A very high tolerance for emotional pain, but this went beyond anything she'd ever imagined. Even the news that her mother unexpectedly succumbed to her cancer didn't touch it. Maybe because she'd prepared herself for that loss, she was able to get through it without falling apart, but in truth, she was pretty sure her heart was too broken to feel it.

At least dealing with the funeral and out-of-town family gave her something to concentrate on besides the betrayal she'd suffered. Moving like a robot, she went through the motions of making arrangements while all three of her brothers stood as an honor guard around her.

Nic hadn't been sure of his reception, but she didn't blame him for bringing Gideon's lies to her attention. Nic understood how unacceptable and wrong hiding the truth was. He'd been right to force it into the light.

As for the man she had thought of as her husband, she saw him once. He came to the service, not making any effort to approach her, but she felt his eyes on her the whole time.

After the first glimpse, she couldn't bear to look at him. All she could think about was how easy she'd been for him in every way, screwing up her courage to propose. Giving in to hormones and his deft proficiency with the female body. Feeling so proud to have a man at all, especially one who made women envy her. He'd played on all her biggest weaknesses, right up to his supposed shared pain over the miscarriages.

Here her heart stalled, torn apart by the idea he'd been faking his grief. It was too unfair, too cruel. Was even a shred of what he'd told her about his childhood true?

That thought weakened her, making her susceptible to excusing his behavior, so she cut herself off from considering it. She'd leaned on Theo's wide chest and focused on the inappropriate dress worn by Demitri's date. Leave it to her youngest brother to bring an escort to his mother's funeral.

Her brothers coped in very different ways, but they stayed close, protective in their way, getting her through those first few weeks of loss so she didn't have to dwell on the fact her marriage had been an unmitigated fraud.

But solitude arrived when they went back to work and Nic went home with his wife and baby.

Adara had to say one thing about her fake of a husband. He'd provoked a new sense of responsibility in both her younger brothers. Demitri was still a wild card, but he hadn't missed a single appointment in his calendar since he'd been informed of her pregnancy, and while she wasn't always comfortable with his newfangled marketing campaigns, they seemed to be working.

As for Theo, well, the middle child was always a dark horse, keeping things inside. Epitomizing the strong silent type, he didn't socialize or like people much at all. That's why she was so surprised when he dropped by the penthouse on his way home from the airport, took off his jacket and asked if he could make himself coffee.

"I can make it," she offered.

"Stay off your feet."

She made a face at his back, tired of a lifetime of being bossed by men, but also tired in general. Elevating her ankles again as she'd been instructed, she went back to studying a spreadsheet on her laptop.

"Why are you working?" he asked when he came back to pace her living room restlessly, steaming cup in his hand.

"I'm not checking up on you, if that's what you think."

"Go ahead. You won't find any mistakes. I don't make them."

She lifted her brows at his arrogance, but he only held her gaze while he sipped his coffee.

"We were never allowed to, were we?" he added with a lightness that had an inner band of steel belting.

Her first instinct was to duck. Were they really going there?

An unavoidable voicing of the truth had emerged in her dealings with her siblings once she'd pulled Nic back into their lives. With the absence of their mother's feelings to worry about, perhaps they were all examining the effects of silence, asking questions that might hurt but cleansed ancient wounds.

"No, only Demitri was allowed. And he made

enough for all of us," she added caustically, stating another unspoken truth.

Theo agreed to that with a pull of one corner of his mouth before he paced another straight line across her wall of windows. "Which leaves me wondering if I should let you make this one."

Adara set aside her laptop and folded her hands over her belly. "Which one is that?"

"The same one our father made."

A *zing* of alarm went through her, more like a paralyzing shock from a cattle prod, actually, leaving her limbs feeling loose and not her own. She clumsily swung her feet to the floor but didn't have the strength to stand.

"If you're talking about Gid—that man who pretended to be my husband, he *lied*, Theo. That's why our father was the way he was. Because Mother betrayed him. Trust me when I tell you it leaves a bitterness you can't rinse out of your mouth." Her heart ached every day with loss and anger and hurt.

"Our father was a twisted, cruel bastard because he never forgave her. Is that what you're going to do? Punish Gideon and take it out on his baby?"

Adara set her hand protectively on her belly.

"Of course not!" She wasn't being that cutting and heartless. Was she?

"Are you going to let him see his child, then?"

She swallowed, unable to say a clear yes or no. The thought of seeing Gideon made her go both hot and cold, burning with anticipation and freezing her with fear that he'd hurt her all over again. She couldn't bear the thought of facing him, knowing how he'd tricked her while part of her still loved the man she'd thought of as her husband. Deep down she knew she couldn't deny her child its father, but the reality of sharing custody with a charlatan was too much to contemplate.

Therefore, she was ignoring the need to make a decision, putting it off until she couldn't avoid it any longer.

"He'll always be in your life in one way or another. Are you going to twist the knife every chance you get? Or act like a civilized human being about it?"

"Stop it," she said, hating the way he was painting her as small and vindictive. He didn't understand how shattering it was to have your perceptions exploded like this. How much like grief it was to lose the man you loved not to an accident, but to duplicity. She rocked herself off the sofa and onto her feet. "Why are you defending him? What do you expect me to do? Lie down and let him wipe his feet on me the way our mother did? He abused my trust!"

"But he didn't abuse you. Did he?" It was a real question, one with a rare thread of uncertainty woven into his tone.

"Of course not," she muttered, instantly repelled by even the suggestion. Why? What did she care what other people thought of Gid—that man?

"You make it sound like you wouldn't have stood for it, but we all hung around for it," Theo pointed out bluntly.

She didn't answer. There was nothing to say to that ugly truth. If she could see her toes, she knew they'd have been curled into the carpet.

"I was scared for you, you know," Theo said gruffly. "When you married him. We didn't know him, who he was, what he was capable of. I watched him like a hawk, and I would have stepped in if he'd made one wrong move, but he didn't. And you..." He narrowed his eyes. "You changed. It took me a while to figure out what was different, but you weren't scared anymore. Were you?"

Adara swallowed, thinking back to those first weeks and months of marriage, when she had been waiting for the other shoe to drop. Gradually she'd begun to trust that the even temper her husband showed her was real. If the ground was icy, he steadied her. If a cab was coming, he drew her back.

And she remembered very clearly the last time her father had touched her in anger, a few weeks after her wedding. She'd been trying to explain why the engineer needed to make changes to a drawing and he'd batted the pencil from her hand, clipping her wrist with his knuckles.

Mere seconds later, Gideon had walked into the room, arriving to take her home.

Her father had changed before her eyes, remaining as blustery as always, but becoming slightly subdued, eyeing her uneasily as she retrieved her pencil and subtly massaged her wrist.

She hadn't said a word, of course, merely confirmed with her father that they were finished for the day before she'd left with Gideon, but she'd realized she had a champion in her husband, passive and ignorant though he was to his role. As long as she had him, she had protection. Her father had never got physical with her again.

That sense of security had become precious to her. That's why she'd been so devastated when she had thought Lexi had snatched him from her, and now the hurt was even worse, when she knew his shielding tenderness had never existed at all.

"It was in his best interest to keep me happy," she said, voice husky and cold. "I was the facade that made him look real."

"Maybe," Theo agreed, twisting the knife that seemed lodged in her own heart. "In the beginning. But... Adara, I would have done everything I could to help you through this pregnancy regardless of any threats from Gideon. You're my sister. I know what this baby means to you. But the way he spoke to me when he called, that was not just a father speaking. He was worried about both of you. Protective. I've always had a healthy respect for him, but I was intimidated that day. There was no way I was going to be the weak link that caused anything to happen to you or this baby."

"Welcome to my world where you buy the snake oil and convince yourself it works," she scoffed.

He stopped his pacing to stare accusingly at her. "You fooled me, you know. Both of you. I looked at how happy you two were in the last few months and I was *hopeful*. I thought finally one of us was shaking off our childhood and making a proper life for herself. You made me start to believe it was possible, and now—"

"He *lied,* Theo."

"Maybe he had reason to," he challenged and moved to retrieve an envelope from the pocket of his raincoat. He dropped it on the coffee table in front of her. "That's from Nic. He asked me to come through on my way back from Tokyo and bring it to you. I didn't read it, but Nic pointed out that he changed his own name to escape his childhood so he shouldn't have judged Gideon for doing it. Maybe you shouldn't, either."

"He didn't convince Nic he'd married him, did he? He didn't sleep with Nic and make him believe in a fantasy!" He hadn't resuscitated Nic's heart back to life only to crush it under his boot heel. She could never, ever forget that.

"He didn't take over the hotels the way he could have," Theo challenged. "If anything, he kept us afloat until now, when we're finally undoing the damage our father did. He could have robbed us blind the minute the will was read. We all owe him for not doing that. I haven't slept," Theo added gruffly. "Call me later if you want any clarification on that balance sheet for Paris."

He left her staring at the envelope that seemed less snake oil and more snake, coiled in a basket and ready to strike the moment she disturbed the contents.

*Throw it in the incinerator,* she thought. Theo didn't know what he was talking about. The difference here was that their mother had loved and lied while Gideon had purely lied. He didn't love her. That final, odd comment he'd made about his ability to love not being in question had been a last-ditch effort to cling to the life he had built *no matter what he had to do.*

Thinking of their child growing up in the same hostile atmosphere she'd known made her stomach turn, though. She didn't want to wield her sense of betrayal like a weapon, damaging everyone close to her.

Maybe if she understood why he'd done it, she'd hate him less. Theo was right about Gideon always being connected to her, no matter how awkward that would be. She would have to rise above her bitterness and learn to be civil to him.

Lowering to the sofa, she opened the envelope and shook out the printed screen shots of clippings and police reports and email chains. Through the next hours she combed through the pieces Nic had gathered, fitting them into a cracked, bleak image of a baby born from a girl abused by her stepfather. The girl's mother had thrown her out when she became pregnant. A ragtag community of dockworkers, social services and street people had tried to help the adolescent keep herself and her beloved son clothed and fed.

It seemed Gideon had been truthful about one thing: his mother had possessed a strong maternal instinct. Delphi had been urged more than once to put him up for adoption, but was on record as stating no one could love him as much as she did. While not always successful at keeping a roof over their heads, she'd done all a girl of her age could, working every low-end, unsavory job possible without resorting to selling drugs or sex.

Sadly, a nasty element working the docks had decided she didn't have to accept money for her body. It could be taken anyway. Adara cried as she read how the young woman had met such a violent end. She cried even harder, thinking of a young boy seeing his mother like that, beaten and raped and left to die.

Blowing her nose, she moved on to the account of Delphi's friends from low places doing the improbable: going to the police and demanding a search for Delphi's son. Here Nic had done the legwork on a trail that the police had let go cold. Taking the thin thread of Delphi's last name, he had tied it to a crew list from a freighter ship dated years later. The name Vozaras was there too, but the first name was Kristor.

A side story took off on a tangent about smuggling, but nothing had been proven. The only charges considered had been for underage labor and somehow that had been dropped.

Adara wiped at a tickle on her cheek as she absorbed the Dickensian tale of a boy who should have been in school, learning and being loved by a family. He'd been aboard a freighter instead, doing the work of a man. No wonder he was such a whiz with all things sea related. He had literally grown up on a ship.

Considering the deprivation he'd known, the loss

of his mother and lack of—as he'd told her himself once—anyone caring about him, it was a wonder he'd turned into a law-abiding citizen at all. When she thought of all the little ways he had looked out for her, even before Greece, when he'd do those small things like make sure she was under the umbrella or huge things like finagle her into running the hotel chain despite her father's interference from the grave, she was humbled.

Perhaps he had been self-serving when he'd agreed to marry her, but he'd treated her far better than the man who was supposed to love and care for her ever had.

She'd been avoiding thinking back to Greece and all that had happened since, but she couldn't ignore his solicitude and protectiveness any longer. He could have let her risk her neck climbing down that cliff alone; he could have sent her to her brother's alone. His actions had gone above and beyond those of a man only wanting to manipulate.

And when she recalled the warmth in his smile when he'd gazed at Evie, the pained longing in him when he'd talked about the loss of their own babies...

Even after that, when they'd been waiting out this pregnancy here, more than once she had glanced up unexpectedly and found a smile of pride softening his face. Half the time his eyes were on her bulging stomach, not even aware she was looking at him. Other times he was looking at her and always seemed to grin a bit ruefully after, as if he'd been caught in a besotted moment and felt sheepish for it.

He couldn't fake all of that. Could he? His shattered control, just from touching her that last night, hadn't been the response of a man who was unmoved and repulsed. He'd been as swept away as she had. Laughing, teasing, pulling her into him afterward as though she was his cherished stuffie.

She swallowed.

Theo was right about a few things. Despite the lack of a truly legal marriage, Gideon had been behaving like a husband and father so well, even she had believed they had a chance for a lifetime of true happiness.

Perhaps they had.

If she hadn't ruined it by throwing him out for daring to reveal the darkest secrets closest to his soul.

She bit her lip, distantly aware of the physical pain, but the emotional anguish was far sharper. It wasn't fair to imagine there had been another time in their lives when they'd been close enough to risk telling each other something so deeply personal. Look how long she'd masked that her father was a brute. If Gideon hadn't followed her to Greece, she might never have told him about that last miscarriage. He'd had as much right to know about their loss as she had to know his name.

Oh, God.

Scanning the scattered papers with burning eyes, she wondered if he even knew this much about himself. She hurt so badly for him, completely understanding why he'd wanted to escape being the boy who had gone through all this and become someone else.

She hadn't even given him a chance to tell his side of things. She *was* just like their father—a man she had never forgiven for the hurts he'd visited on all of them.

But after acting just like him, she couldn't ask Gideon for another chance. Not when he'd taken such a huge risk and she'd condemned him for it.

How could she expect him to forgive her when she'd never forgive herself?

It killed Gideon to do it, but he put together the necessary declaration of his identity and the rest of what was needed to dissolve their fake marriage. Then he had the paperwork couriered to the penthouse.

Adara wasn't taking his calls. The least he could do was make things easier on her. Karen was reporting that everything was progressing fine, but all he could think was that Adara must be devastated by the loss of her mother on top of what he'd done to her. He was eating his heart out, aching every moment of every day, but he couldn't badger her for a chance to explain himself. What was there to explain? He'd lied.

He wasn't her husband.

So why was he personally reframing the apartment below their penthouse, executing the plans his architect had drawn up once they'd decided to stay in the city and expand their living space to two floors, creating a single master bedroom with a nursery off the side?

Because he was a fool. It was either this or climb

on the next boat and never touch land again. The option kept tapping him on the shoulder, but for some reason he couldn't bring himself to take it.

He couldn't be that far away from the woman he regarded as his wife.

He stopped hammering, chest vibrating with the hollowness of loss.

Actually, that was his cell phone, buzzing in his pocket.

Setting aside the hammer, he saw the call was from Adara. His heart stopped as he hurried to remove his leather glove and accept the call.

"Babe?" The endearment left his lips as if he was sleeping beside her.

Nothing. Damn, he'd missed it. He started to lower the phone and reconnect, but heard a faint "You said you'd be here."

"What?" He brought the phone to his ear.

"You said I wouldn't have to go through this alone and that you'd be with me every second and the pains have started but *you're not here*. You lied about that too."

Adrenaline singed a path through his arteries and exploded in his heart. "You're in labor?"

A sniff before she gritted out a resentful "Yes."

He threw off his hard hat and safety goggles. "Where are you?"

Silence.

"Adara!"

"In the apartment," she groused. "And you're not."

"Where in the apartment?" he demanded, running up the emergency stairs two at a time to the service entrance. "Don't scream if you hear someone in the kitchen. It's me. Did you change the code?"

"What? How are you in the kitchen? I'm in the bed—" She sucked in a breath.

He stabbed the keypad and the light went green.

He shot through the door, into the kitchen, and strode to her room, ears pounding at the silence. Her bedroom looked like a crime scene with clothes tossed everywhere, nylons bunched on the floor, slippers strewn into the corner, but no Adara. He checked the bathroom.

"Where are you?" he demanded.

"Here," she insisted in his ear. "By the bed."

He'd been on both sides of her bed and rounded it again, but she wasn't there. "Damn it, Adara."

He lowered the phone and shouted, "Where *are* you?"

"Here!" she screamed.

Her voice came from the other side of the penthouse. He ran through the living room to his room. *Their* room. A faint part of him wanted to read something significant into that, but when he entered, he didn't see her there either.

Was she torturing him on purpose—?

*Oh, hell.* He spotted one white fist clinging to the rumpled blanket. Her dark head was bent against the far side of the mattress.

"Oh, babe," he said, and threw his phone aside to come around to where she knelt, bare shoulders rising and falling with her panting breaths. She had a towel around her, but nothing else. Her hair was dripping wet.

"Okay, I'm here. You're sure this is just labor?"

"I know what labor feels like, Gideon."

"Okay, okay," he soothed. "Can I get you onto the bed?" He was afraid to touch her. "Are you bleeding?"

"No, but my water broke. That's why I had a shower." She kept her forehead buried against the side of the mattress. "I'm not ready for this. It hurts. And I'm so scared the baby will die—"

"Shh, shh." He stroked her cold shoulder with a shaky hand. "Have you felt the baby move?"

She nodded. "But anything could happen."

"Nothing is going to happen. I'm right here." He prayed to God he wasn't lying to her about this. Shakily he picked up her phone and ended their call. "Have you called the ambulance? Karen?"

"No." She swiped her eyes on her bare arm, and peeked over her elbow at him, gaze full of dark vulnerability and a frightened longing that put pressure on his lungs. "I just thought of you, that you said you'd be here with me. Where were you? How did you get here so fast?"

"Downstairs," he answered, dialing Karen's personal line from memory. In seconds he had briefed her and ended the call. "She'll meet us at the hospital. An ambulance is on the way."

"Oh, leave it to you to get everything done in one call."

"Are you complaining?" He eased her to her feet and onto the bed, muscles twitching to draw her cold, damp skin against him to warm her up, but he drew the covers over her instead. Sitting beside her on the bed, he rested one hand on the side of her neck and stared into her eyes. "You know me. I won't settle for anything less than the best."

*Her,* he was not so subtly implying.

Her brow wrinkled and her mouth trembled. She looked away.

Now wasn't the time to break through the walls she'd put up between them though. He reluctantly drew away and stood.

"Where are you going?" she asked with alarm.

"Have you packed a bag?"

"No, but... You're coming with me, aren't you?" she asked as he moved to find an empty overnight case. "To the hospital?"

"You couldn't keep me away. Not even if you had me arrested." She must have wanted to. Why hadn't she? He glanced over and her hand was outstretched to him, urging him with convulsive clasps to return to her side. Her expression strained into silent agony.

He leaped toward her and grabbed her hand, letting her cling to him as he breathed with her through the contraction, keeping her from hyperventilating, staring into her eyes with as much confidence as he could possibly instill while hiding how much her pain distressed him. He hated seeing her suffer. This was going to kill him.

She released a huge breath and let go of his hand to throw her arm over her eyes. "I'm being a weakling about this. I'm sorry."

"Don't," he growled. Her apology made him want to drop to his knees and beg her for forgiveness. He packed instead, throwing in one of his shirts as a nightgown, a pair of her stretchy sweats, her toothbrush and the moisturizer she always used. "Slippers, hairbrush, lip balm. What else?"

Adara watched him move economically through the space they'd shared, demonstrating how well he knew her as he unhesitatingly gathered all the things she used every day: vitamins, hair clips, even the lozenges she kept by the bed for if she had a cough in the night.

"I—" *read about your mother,* she wanted to say, but another pain ground up from the middle of her spine to wrap around her bulging middle. She gritted her teeth and he took her hand, reassuring her with a steady stare of unwavering confidence and command of the moment, silently willing her to accept and ride and wait for it to release her from its grip.

His focus allowed her to endure the pain without panic. As the contraction subsided, she fell back on the pillow again, breathing normally.

"Those are close," he said, glancing at the clock.

"They started hours ago. I was in denial."

She got a severe look for that, but he was distracted from rebuking her by the arrival of the paramedics. Minutes later, she was strapped to a gurney, her hand well secured in Gideon's sure grasp as she was taken downstairs and loaded into the ambulance.

From there, nothing existed but the business of delivering a baby. As promised, Gideon stayed with her every second. And he was exactly the man she'd always known—the one who seemed to know what she wanted or needed the moment it occurred to her. When the lights began to irritate her, he had them lowered. When she was examined, he shooed extra people from the room, sensitive to her inherent modesty. He kept ice chips handy and gathered her sweaty hair off her neck and never flinched once, no matter how tightly she gripped his arm or how colorfully she swore and blamed him for the pain she was in.

"I can't do it," she sobbed at one point, so exhausted she wanted to die.

"Think of how much you hate me," he cajoled.

She didn't hate him. She wanted to, but she couldn't. She loved him too much.

But she was angry with him. He'd hurt her so badly. It went beyond anything she had imagined she could endure. And then she'd found out *why* he'd lied and it made her hate herself. She was angry most about his leaving her. Living without him was a wasteland of numbness punctuated with spikes of remembered joy that froze and faded as soon as they were recalled. He'd left her in that agonizing state for weeks and…

Another pain built and she gathered all her fury and betrayal, letting it knot her muscles and feed her strength and then she *pushed…*

Gideon stood with his feet braced on the solid floor, but swayed as though a deck rocked beneath him. His son, swaddled into a tight roll by an efficient nurse, wore a disgruntled red face. He wouldn't be satisfied with the soothing sway much longer, not when his tiny stomach was empty. He kept his eyes stubbornly shut, but let out an angry squawk and turned his head to root against the edge of the blanket.

Why that made Gideon want to laugh and cry at the same time, he didn't know. Maybe because he was overtired. He hadn't slept, his body felt as if he'd been thrown down a flight of stairs, his skin had the film of twenty-four hours without a shower and his own stomach was empty. This was like a hangover, but a crazy good one that left him unable to hold on to clear thoughts. And even though he had a sense he should be filled with regret, he was so elated it was criminal.

"I know, son," he whispered against the infant's unbelievably tender cheek. "But Mama is so tired. Can you hang on a little longer, till she wakes up?" He tried a different pattern of jiggling and offered a fingertip only to have it rejected with a thrust of the baby's tongue.

The boy whimpered a little more loudly.

"I'm awake," Adara said in the sweet, sleepy voice he'd been missing like a limb from his body.

Gideon turned from the rain beyond the window and found her lying on her side, her hand tucked under the side of her face as she watched him. The tender look in her eyes filled him with such unreasonable hope, he had to swallow back a choked sob. He consciously shook off the dream that tried to balloon in his head. *Get real,* he told himself, recalling why he was missing her so badly. His heart plummeted as though he'd taken a steel toe into it.

"He's hungry?" she asked.

"Like he's never been fed a day in his life."

Adara smirked and glanced at the clock, noting the boy was barely four hours into his life. With some wincing and a hand from Gideon, she pulled herself to sit up.

"Sore?" He glanced toward the door, thinking to call a nurse.

"It's okay. He's worth it." She got her arm out of the sleeve of her gown, exposing her swollen breast.

"Do you, um, want to cover up with something?" He looked around for a towel.

"Why?" She drew the edge of her gown across her chest again. "Is there someone else in here?"

"No, just me."

"Oh, well, that's okay then, isn't it?" She started

to reveal herself again, but hesitated, her confused gaze striking his with shadows of such deep uncertainty, his heart hurt.

"Of course it's okay." He wanted to lean down and kiss her, he was so moved that she still felt so natural around him. It could only mean good things, couldn't it?

Adara could hardly look into Gideon's eyes, but she couldn't look away. He delved so searchingly into her gaze, as if looking for confirmation they stood a chance, but she'd treated him so badly, rejecting him for being as self-protective as she'd always been. She didn't know how to bridge this chasm between them.

Their son found his voice with an insistent yell and made them both start.

And then, even though she'd had a brief lesson before falling asleep, Adara had to learn to breast-feed, which wasn't as natural a process as some mothers made it look. She wasn't sure how to hold him. Her breast was too swollen for such a tiny mouth.

Their son surpassed his patience and grew too fussy to try. Gideon looked at her with urgency to get the job done as the baby began to wail in earnest.

"What am I doing wrong?" she cried.

"Don't look at me, I've never done it either. Here, I'll sit beside you and hold him so you can line him up— There, see? He's never done it, either, but he's getting it."

She didn't know what was more stingingly sweet: the first pull of her baby's mouth on her nipple or the stirring way Gideon cradled her against his chest so he could help her hold their baby. Adara blinked back tears, frantically wondering how she could be so close to Gideon and feel he was so far out of reach at the same time.

She tensed to hide that she was beginning to tremble, finding words impossible as emotion overwhelmed her. At least she had her back tucked to his chest and he couldn't see her face.

He seemed to react to her tension, pulling away with a grimace that he smoothed from his expression before she'd properly glimpsed it. Standing by the bed with his hands in the pockets of his rumpled work pants, he stared at the baby.

She did too, not knowing where else to look, then became fascinated by the miracle of a closed fist against her breast, tiny lashes, the peek of a miniature earlobe from beneath the edge of the blue cap.

A drop of pure emotion fell from her eye, landing on his cheek.

"Oh," she gasped, drying the betraying tear. "I'm just so overwhelmed," she said, trying to dismiss that she was crying over a lot more than the arrival of their son.

"I know." Gideon's blurred image took a step forward and he gestured helplessly. "I didn't expect it to be like this."

*Like this.* Those words seemed to encompass a lot more than a safe delivery after so many heartaches.

Adara blinked, trying to clear her vision to see what was in his face, eyes, heart, but all she could think was that she'd screwed up and thrown away something unbelievably precious. Her eyes flooded with despondent tears.

"Please come home," she choked out. "With us. We won't be a family without you and I miss you so much—" She couldn't continue.

"Oh, babe." He rushed forward, his warm hand cupping her face as he settled his hip beside her thigh and drew her into him, pressing hot lips against her temple, her wet cheek, her trembling lips. "I've been trying to think how I'd ever convince you to let me. I'm *sorry.*"

She shook her head, burying her face in the hollow of his shoulder as she tried to regain control. "It's okay." She sniffed. "It was never easy for me to tell you about my childhood horrors. I shouldn't have expected you to revisit yours without some serious prodding."

He massaged the back of her head, his chin rubbing her hair. "I didn't want to, but mostly because I knew it could be the breaking point of our marriage. I didn't want that. And not because it would expose me. I didn't want to lose *you.* Does it help at all to know that I've always felt married to you? Maybe it wasn't legal, but it was real to me. You're my wife, Adara."

She nodded. "I am."

He laughed a little, the sound one of husky joy. "You are." He drew back, cupping her face as he looked for confirmation in her eyes. "You are."

She bit her lips, holding back the longing as she nodded. "I am. It's enough."

The radiant pride in his expression dimmed. "Enough?"

"Knowing that our union matters to you. That you want me as your wife. That we can be a family."

He sat back, hands falling away from her. "What are you saying? What does all of that do for you?"

"What do you mean? It's good, Gideon. I want to carry on as we were, treating this like a real marriage. We don't have to change anything or bring up your past or involve any lawyers. My brothers know why we separated, but no one else does. You are Gideon Vozaras. I'm Mrs. Vozaras. It's all good."

He stood abruptly, his mood shifting to acute dismay. "And why are you staying married to that man? That name?"

"Because—" *I love him.* Her heart dipped. She wasn't ready to put herself out there again and get nothing in return. "There's no point in shaking things up. I read those papers you sent and they say that I have a case to take you to the cleaners, but I don't want that. I'm fine with us being married in a common-law sort of way. No use rocking the boat." There, she was using language he understood.

Or should, but his jaw was like iron as he moved to the window and showed her a scant angle of his profile and a tense line across his shoulders.

"You asked me if we were falling in love," he reminded.

"It was never part of our deal. I can live without it," she hurried to say.

"I can't."

His words plunged a knife into her. She gasped and looked wildly around as she absorbed what it could mean if he wanted a marriage based on love, but was stuck with her—

"For God's sake, Adara. Are you still not seeing what you mean to me?" He was looking over his shoulder at her, incredulous, but incredibly gentle too.

"What?" Her breast was cold and she realized the baby had fallen asleep and let her nipple slip from his mouth. She wished for extra hands as she tried to cradle the baby and cover herself at the same time.

Gideon walked over and grasped her chin, forcing her gaze up to his. A fire burned in the back of that intense gaze, one that sparked an answering burn in her.

She still wasn't sure, though…

"You're not bound to me legally, but that doesn't matter if I own your heart," he told her. "I want you, body and soul. If there's something standing in the way of your loving me, tell me what it is. Now. So I can fix it or remove it and have you once and for all."

"I—" She almost lost her nerve, but sensed it really was time to let go of the last of her insecurities and be open about what she wanted. Grasp it. Demand it. "I want you to love me back."

She wasn't just wearing her heart on her sleeve, she'd pinned it to the clothesline and wheeled it out into the yard.

A look of unbelievable tenderness softened his harsh expression. "How could I not?"

She slowly shook her head. "Don't make it sound like it's there just like that. I was awful to you. I know that you've lost people close to you and don't want to be hurt again. It's okay that you're not able to love me yet. I can wait." Maybe. She set her chin, determined it wouldn't tremble despite the fact her heart was in her throat.

If only he wasn't so confusing, smiling indulgently at her like that.

"You do love me." He cradled the side of her face in his palm, scanning her face as if he was memorizing it, and she suddenly realized she must look like something the cat had coughed up. Her hair hadn't been washed, she'd barely rinsed her mouth with a sip of water.

Self-consciously she lifted the baby to her shoulder and rubbed his back, using him as a bit of a shield while she worked at maintaining hold of her emotions.

"I love you quite a bit, actually," she confessed toward her blanket-covered knees. "It's not anything like what I feel for the other men in my life. This one included." She hitched the baby a bit higher and couldn't resist kissing his little cheek, even as her soul reached out to his father. "I don't know how to handle what I feel for you. When my father was mean to me, it hurt even though I didn't care about him, but it's nothing compared to how much it hurts when you love someone and trust him and think they don't care about you at all."

"I know," he growled. "Losing someone to death is agony, but it's even worse knowing the person you love with all your heart is alive and doesn't want to see you."

Hearing how much he loved her was bitter-sweet. She stared at him in anguish, not wanting the power to hurt him that badly, but seeing from his tortured expression that she had. There were no words to heal, only an urge to draw him close so she could try to kiss away his pain.

"I'm sorry. I love you."

"I know, me, too. I love you so much."

Their mouths met in homecoming, both of them moaning as the ache ceased. He opened his lips over hers and she flowered like a plant tasting water. Heat flowed into her. Joy.

*Love.*

A door swished and a nurse said, "Bit soon for that, isn't it?"

They broke apart. Gideon shot a private smile at Adara as he reached to tie her gown behind her neck.

"And how is our young man? Does he have a name?" the nurse chattered.

Adara licked her lips, eyeing Gideon as she said, "Delphi's not exactly a boy's name, but I thought... Androu?" It was Gideon's real name.

His expression spasmed with emotion before

he controlled it. "Are you sure?" he asked, voice strained, body braced for disappointment.

"He's someone I love and want in my life forever. I think, someday, he'd be really proud to know who he was named after."

"I don't deserve you," he said against her lips, kissing her resoundingly, right there in front of the nurse.

Adara flushed and smiled, bubbles of happiness filling her. "We do, you know," she contradicted him. "We both deserve this."

She didn't care that the nurse was smiling indulgently at them even as she took Androu and undressed him so she could weigh him.

"Well, you certainly deserve to be happy. Me, I just demand the best and get it." *You,* he mouthed. *Him.* He cocked his head toward the baby.

"A habit I'm adopting," she said with a cheeky wrinkle of her nose. "I know how possessive you are of the things you've built, too. I'm taking on that trait as well. *Us,*" she whispered, soft and heartfelt.

"Yeah, I'm going to hang on to us pretty tight too," he said in a way that made her heart leap. *"Agape mou."*

# EPILOGUE

GIDEON WALKED INTO his home office thinking he really needed to start spending more time in here. It wasn't that things were falling apart. He and Adara had put some great people in place when they'd first learned of the pregnancy. Her brothers were still running things like a well-oiled machine and he should have quit micromanaging years ago, so this was a timely lesson in letting go.

But there was a fine line between delegating and neglecting. Much more lolling about his home, playing airplane with his son and necking with his wife, and he'd be a full-fledged layabout.

Of course, he could blame finishing the renovations, putting in a staircase to the lower floor, painting and furnishing their new private space away from the main floor. That had taken time. There had also been his recovery from minor surgery, but that had really only been the one afternoon on headache pills and he'd been fine.

No, he might be getting up in the night to change diapers, but he wasn't breast-feeding or anemic from childbirth. He didn't have Adara's totally legitimate reasons for shirking work.

He certainly shouldn't be leaving confidential papers lying openly on his desk, whether the workmen were gone or not.

The block letters and signature tabs were a dead giveaway that this was a contract, one he couldn't remember even pulling out to review, but— Ah. It was the separation agreement he'd sent to Adara. She must have left it here.

A pang hit him, but it was merely the remembered pain of thinking he'd lost everything and was quickly relieved by a rush of relief and happiness that they'd recovered. Her devotion was as steadfast as his, prompting a flood of deep love for her as he walked the papers toward the shredder. He didn't want this bad mojo in the house, but then he saw she'd signed it. His heart stopped.

Ha. That wasn't her name. Under the statement that began, *I, Adara Makricosta, hereby agree...* she'd scrawled with a deep impression, *Never,* and added a smiley face.

Quirking a grin at her sass, he decided this was

a signed contract in its own right, definitely worth tucking in the safe. Suddenly, work didn't seem important after all. Was she finished feeding Androu? he wondered. They'd had coinciding follow-ups at separate doctor clinics today. He'd returned to find her rocking a drifting Androu to sleep downstairs and decided to see what he could get done here, but…

He turned to find her in his office doorway, the baby monitor in her hand.

"He's asleep?" he asked.

She nodded and came to set the monitor on his desktop. "How did your appointment go?"

"Not swimmingly."

Her eyes widened in alarm.

"That's a joke," he hurried to assure her. "I'm saying there were no swimmers. I'm good. Shooting blanks."

She snorted, then sobered and cocked her head in concern. "You're sure it doesn't bother you? I really was fully prepared to have my tubes tied."

He tried to wave away the same worries he'd been trying to alleviate for weeks, but she kept her anxious expression.

He sighed. "I'd make ten more just like Androu

if we could. We both would, right? He's perfect," he said, moving to take her arms in a warm but firm grasp of insistence. "But if we want more children, we can find another way. You can't risk another pregnancy."

"Exactly why I should have been the one having the permanent procedure. What if someday—"

"Are you going somewhere?" he challenged lightly. "I'm not. Therefore, my getting fixed is a solution for both of us. You've been through enough. And this was not a big moral struggle for me. I'm happy to take responsibility for protecting you."

She pouted a little. "Well, thank you then. I do appreciate it."

He caressed from the base of her throat to under her chin, coaxing her to tilt her head up so he could see those pillowy lips pursed so erotically.

"There was some self-serving to it, you know," he admitted, voice thickening with the many weeks of abstinence they'd observed. Now there'd never be any worries for either of them, no matter when or where they came together. And hell, if he hadn't inflicted pain down there to distract himself, he probably would have lost his mind waiting for this moment. "How did *your* appointment go?" he belatedly asked, reminding himself not to let the engine rev too high and fast.

"Oh." Her lashes swooped and her mouth widened into a sensual smile of invitation. "All clear to resume normal activities."

"If you can call how we make each other feel 'normal.'" He backed her toward the desk. "I was just thinking I haven't been spending enough quality time in here."

Her breath caught in the most delightful way, and even though she stiffened in surprise when her hips met the edge of his desk, she melted with reception just as quickly, hitching herself to sit on it. Her hand curled around to the back of his neck and she leaned her other hand onto the surface of his desk, watching without protest as he began unbuttoning her top.

"We do have a nice new bed downstairs that hasn't been used for one of its intended purposes, you know," she reminded in a sultry voice.

"I am quite aware," he countered dryly as he bared her chest and released her bra. Her breasts were bigger, pale and lightly veined, the nipples dark and stiff with excitement. "God, you're beautiful."

"They're kind of majestic, aren't they?" She arched a little.

"They kind of are," he agreed with awe, tracing lightly before he bent to touch careful kisses around her nipples.

"Gideon?"

Her tone made him raise his head. "What's wrong?"

"I know we should savor this because it's been a really long time and we kind of started over with our marriage so this is a bit of a honeymoon moment, but I've really missed making love with you. I thought about walking in here naked. I don't want to wait."

Ever willing to accommodate, he stripped her pants off without another word, taking her ice-blue undies with them. Spreading her knees, he only bothered to open his jeans and shove them down as far as necessary, before he carefully pushed inside her.

Adara gasped at the pinch and friction of not being quite ready, but his hot, firm thickness was the connection she'd been longing for. With a moan, she twined her legs around him and forced his entry, drawing a deep hiss from him.

They fought a light battle, him trying to slow her down, her urging him as deep into her as she could take before she sprawled back on his desk and let him have his way with her.

It was raw and quick and powerful, over in minutes, but they were shaking in each other's arms as they caught their breath. Her vision sparkled and she felt as if she radiated ecstasy.

"You okay?" he murmured as he kissed her neck. "That was pretty primal."

"That was an appetizer," she said, languidly kissing him and using her tongue. Her fingertips traced the damp line through his shirt down his spine. "*Now* you can take me downstairs and show me your best moves."

"You're sounding pretty bossy there, Mrs. Vozaras." He straightened and gently disengaged so he could hitch up his jeans and scoop her off the desk into a cradle against his chest.

"Only a problem if we want different things, and I don't think that's true."

He cocked his head in agreement. "You're so right. Monitor," he prompted, dipping his still-weak knees so she could grab it off the corner of the desk.

She craned her neck over his shoulder as he carried her through the door. "You gonna leave my clothes on the floor like that?"

"Do I look stupid? We're on the clock. He could wake up any second."

She traced his lips with her fingertip. "But if the boat rocks, they'll be thrown all over the place," she teased.

He paused on the stairs. "I am dry-docked and landlocked, sticking right here with you, my siren of a wife. We're on solid ground. Nothing is going anywhere."

"Aw." Touched, she kissed him. It grew deeply passionate. He let her legs drift to find the step above him so he could roam his hands over her naked curves, lighting delicious fires in her nerve endings.

She worked on divesting him, caressing heated skin, leaving a few more articles of clothing on the stairs before she led him below to christen their new bed.

* * * * *